I0597774

THE TOWN KILLERS

Jason Manning

This is a work of fiction. Names, characters, businesses, places, events and incidents are either the products of the author's imagination or used in a fictitious manner. Any resemblance to actual persons, living or dead, or actual events is purely coincidental.

This book or any portion thereof may not be reproduced or used in any manner whatsoever without the express written permission of the publisher except for the use of brief quotations in a book review.

The Town Killers Copyright © 2018 Jason Manning
ISBN: 978-1680680713
Published as a service of the Ethan Ellenberg Literary Agency

Cover design by Matt Forsyth

CHAPTER ONE

The Staked Plains

I.

In the autumn of 1875, Cord Remington was riding east with his sister Emma across the Llano Estacado, thinking about how the Comanches had been the rulers of these semi-arid plains for generations—until very recently.

"Some say the Comanche Wars are over," he commented. "But others swear there are still some holdouts." He glanced across at Emma. "I would hate for a bunch of Comanche warriors to get their hands on you. They seemed to have an eye for pretty white women. Just ask Cynthia Ann Parker."

Emma looked at him. She could tell by his tone of voice and the expression on his face that he was worried. "I'm sure I would manage. I mean it couldn't be all bad," she remarked. "As I recall, Cynthia Ann Parker died of a broken heart after being separated from the Comanches."

He knew that his sister was just trying to ease his anxiety with her flippant remark about the treatment she would likely receive at the hands of Comanches. Emma Remington was notoriously open about her aptitude when it came to bedding men. In the Victorian era that was something proper women simply didn't do, even in the West, where immorality, like lawlessness, was easier to get away with. One could make the case that Emma was a young woman of loose morals, and in fact some people had done just that.

She didn't care what others thought about her, but Cord did, and while he might kid her about it, he had also utilized his skills as a former prizefighter to beat some manners into men who insulted his sister. Not that she needed much defending. Emma was supremely capable of taking care of herself.

"Well, that's true," said Cord, steering his lanky bay horse around a small mesquite and noticing a large prairie dog town up ahead and to his right. He estimated it had to be at least twenty acres big, and he wondered how many 'barking squirrels,' as Meriwether Lewis had called these rodents, lived in the town. His sister's comment cheered him up and he decided to kid her right back. "In fact, I doubt the Comanches could handle you." His sister was the smartest and most dangerous woman he knew, and he had met a few.

Emma just laughed. It was just like her to take his comment as a compliment. She angled her red roan to the left, since her brother was intent on giving the prairie dog town a wide berth. Out here, a mount breaking a leg by stepping in a prairie dog hole was quite likely a death warrant for the rider.

A cold blustery wind was blowing in from the north, and Cord pulled his hat down more firmly on his head while turning in the saddle to look check their backtrail. A pack horse was on a long lead tied to his saddle, carrying the provisions they required for the three-week journey across the Staked Plains, including a couple of sacks of corn dodgers, along with beans, flour, coffee, salted beef and a half dozen large water skins, since water was scarce out here. But Cord wasn't checking on the pack horse or the supplies it carried. Instead, he carefully scanned the mesquite plains that seemed to stretch forever in all directions. He hadn't seen another human being for many days now. But that didn't mean there weren't some out there. The gusting winds would disperse any dust kicked up by riders too quickly for him to see it. And since these plains were wild and largely unsettled country, with few towns and army posts to speak of, it was a pretty safe bet that anyone you met in these parts was dangerous.

Just because he saw no indication that they were being followed didn't ease his mind. He had been afflicted all day with an uneasy feeling that their passage through this country had not gone unnoticed. His hunches had been right too many times for him to ignore this one.

Twenty-five years of age, Cord was a lean, rangy, broad-shouldered man who stood six feet tall, with blue-gray eyes that were usually warm and friendly, though they could turn hard as gun metal and cold as glacial ice.

There was a thick and unruly mane of black hair under his stained old campaign hat. Women found him handsome, even with the dark stubble that usually appeared on his cheeks when he was on the trail. He wore a faded blue shirt under a knee-length leather coat, and brown canvas pants made by Levi Strauss tucked into stovepipe boots.

Since Emma had refused to rise to the bait with his nonchalant comment about how she might like the attention of Comanche bucks, they rode in silence for a while, But Cord couldn't be silent for long. It wasn't that he liked to hear himself talk. But his mind was brimming over with knowledge and the ideas that sprang from that knowledge. He absorbed information like sand absorbed raindrops.

"The Comanche troubles probably wouldn't be over yet but for what happened at Tule Canyon. That's where Ranald Mackenzie's 4th Cavalry slaughtered about a thousand Comanche ponies and destroyed most of the tribe's food stores last year."

Emma's brows furrowed. She was a dark-haired beauty of twenty-two summers, with sea-green eyes in a perfectly sculptured and very expressive oval face. She was slender, perhaps a bit too slender to be fashionable. She was taller, too, at five feet, eight inches—just a couple of inches shorter than her brother. She wore black soft-brushed cotton pants, a sun-bleached, pale yellow shirt, and a long brown canvas duster. Her long black tresses were wind-blown.

"That's horrible," she declared. She didn't just use a horse to get from one point to another, she loved them, be they mustangs or thoroughbreds, and she had been riding about as long as she could walk. She was an accomplished trick rider, too. Cord had seen her go quite a long way standing balanced atop a galloping horse. She could ride on one side or the other of the horse's barrel, like Indian warriors did to make themselves as small a target as possible for an enemy. She had won a bet in Hot Springs, Arkansas by sliding down one side of a saddle, completely under a galloping horse, and then climbing back up the other side of the hull.

"Agreed," said Cord, regretting that he had failed to consider his sister's love for horses before mentioning Tule Canyon. "But effective. It wasn't long after that that Quanah Parker—Cynthia Ann's son, by the way—took his Quohada band to Fort Sill and accepted Mackenzie's terms of surrender. He was the last holdout."

All joking aside, Cord figured it was likely there had to be some Comanche renegades still roaming the land and looking for blood. That was why he and

Emma had suffered through some cold night camps on their way east. They would work their way into a likely looking thicket and just lay down on the ground, rolled up in their blankets and go to sleep without risking a campfire.

"We're maybe two, three days away from Wolf Creek," he said. "I don't know about you, but I'm ready for a nice big home-cooked meal."

"I'm ready for a nice hot bath and a soft bed," replied Emma. "In which I don't have to worry about waking up sharing my blankets with a rattlesnake," She glanced at him, smirking. "Or a Comanche." A moment later she said, "And why are we going to Wolf Creek again?"

Cord smiled. Another of his sister's quirks was on display. Emma liked to pretend that she paid little attention to the jobs they were given, that she was somehow above the work they did, and that she was just along for the ride. This attitude had never caused her to give less than one hundred percent effort, however, when it came to *doing* the job.

II.

Three weeks earlier, the job had come to them courtesy of Colonel Ezariah Bronson, U.S. Army. They had met Bronson in a private rail car at Lamy, fifteen miles southeast of Santa Fe, a town they had become familiar with and eventually used as a base when they were doing a lot of jobs in Mexico and the Southwest territories.

The private car was accompanied by a locomotive, a tender and a second car used for stores and luggage and the sleeping quarters of Bronson's aide, Cletus Raine. The car itself contained no ordinary bench seats but rather a round table with six chairs, a desk and chair, a washbasin, several large traveler's trunks and a narrow bed. As a special aide to the Secretary of War, Bronson traveled extensively, by rail when possible, from his base at Fort Leavenworth, Kansas.

Bronson had been a good friend of their father, Silas Remington, and had known Cord and Emma as children. He greeted them like they were his own offspring and engaged in some small talk, asking after their recent exploits in Durango, then inquired if they would like a drink. They gave their orders to Raine, a tall, broad-shouldered Buffalo Soldier who had served with distinction in the 10th Cavalry since its inception and who wore the two chevrons of a corporal on the sleeve of his blue woolen fatigue blouse.

The colonel was a wiry, bewhiskered man in his fifties, a career soldier who had been a callow lieutenant when he fought in the Mexican-American War, and a major when he fought under the command of McClellan, Hooker, Meade and Grant against Robert E. Lee's Army of Northern Virginia during the Civil War, earning a field promotion to colonel at Spotsylvania. He and Silas Remington had become fast friends at West Point

After Captain Silas Remington's death at the hands of Confederate diehards in New Orleans in 1866, Bronson had committed himself to the care of his old friend's two children, as their mother had passed away from cholera when Emma was only four years old. He had put them in the care of his widowed sister, who lived in San Francisco, and Martha Bronson had loved them as she would have her own offspring, had she been able to have any.

Their father's death had been the catalyst for Cord and Emma leaving behind their careers as performers to become detectives. They had traveled to New Orleans and at great risk to their lives eventually tracked down the killers. Bronson had encouraged them to pursue this new vocation because, even though he worried about their well-being, there was no denying that each of them had a unique set of skills that made them eminently qualified.

"I heard you two hunted down Blackie Blackmon up in the Sierra Madres. Ended his twenty-year career of preying on travelers, robbing them, sometimes killing them, and … eating them." His bushy eyebrows arched quizzically. "Is that last part actually true?"

"I believe so," said Cord. "We found a pile of bones near his cabin west of Kings Cabin. Some of the bones were human."

Bronson nodded. Cord had a voracious appetite for knowledge, and knew more than most people on a wide range of topics, so the colonel didn't doubt for one moment that he could distinguish human bones from those of animals.

"Then there's the fact that Blackmon had my brother cooking in a big pot when I killed him," said Emma.

Cord chuckled and told Bronson, "That's *not* true."

"But it sounds exciting, you have to admit," countered Emma.

"As long as the bastard's dead," said Bronson.

"Oh, he's definitely dead," said Emma, emphatically.

"The state of California didn't seem too interested in our bringing him back alive," added Cord. "Not after he wrought havoc on one of the geological survey teams they had sent in to explore and map the mountains."

Raine arrived with a tray bearing their drinks. He proffered the tray to Emma first, and she smiled warmly as she took the Sazerac—cognac and bitters.

"So nice to see you again, Cletus," she said, smiling warmly.

"Nice to see you too, Miss," he replied self-consciously in his gruffly baritone voice, then glanced sheepishly at Bronson, as Cord took his bourbon and the colonel took his scotch whiskey from the tray. If he thought the affection with which Emma Remington greeted his aide was curious, the colonel didn't show it.

"A job well done, then," said Bronson, addressing the Remingtons and as he took a drink he reflected on how proud of his children Silas Remington would have been. Cord and Emma had become the troubleshooters that individuals, companies, states and territories, and even the United States government wanted to hire when they had a problem west of the Mississippi. As a result, the Remington siblings were pretty well off, and they looked it. Emma was wearing an ivory silk day dress with a lined and stayed bodice. A standup collar sported a lace bowtie at the neckline, and the long flowing skirt had a draped overskirt with ruffles and a draped lace tail decorating the bustle. The dress showed off her slender figure to perfection. Cord's black double-breasted frock coat was well-tailored and close-fitting, as was his double-breasted waistcoat with its quilted silk turnover.

Cord and Emma complimented each other quite well with respect to their talents. In addition to being a scholar, Cord was a linguist fluent in Spanish and French and many other languages, and could communicate with the Plains tribes in their native tongues or sign language. He was a card shark to rival Canada Bill Jones and the famous Mississippi riverboat gambler, George Duvol. He was a tough and talented bare-knuckle boxer who had won seventeen of twenty-one bouts in California before he turned twenty, and was said by some to be in the same league as Joe Goss and Jem Mace. And he was quite deadly with the twin Arkansas Toothpicks custom-made to his specifications by James Black just before the famous maker of the Bowie Knife passed away.

Emma was as beautiful as her brother was strikingly handsome. A superb marksman, she engaged in exhibition shooting during the years that her brother was a prizefighter. Promoters touted her as "The Girl Who Couldn't Miss." Together they had frequently performed their various skills at fairs and festivals from Fresno to San Francisco and up and down the Sacramento River. Emma also made a name for herself as a trick rider. Her love for and knowledge of horses knew no bounds. As a tracker, she could rival an Apache. Cord liked to brag that his sister could track an ant across a boulder. In San

Francisco and New Orleans she was a well-known socialite and much sought after by bachelors. But Emma was too much the free spirit to settle for city life. She much preferred roaming the plains and mountains of the West with her brother.

It didn't surprise the colonel that these two young people had earned a name for themselves in a relatively short time. Their father had been both mentally and physically imposing, a well-educated warrior skilled with both pistol and cutlass. He had been a decorated officer who rose swiftly through the ranks, and hand-picked by President Andrew Johnson to help pave the way for the Reconstruction of the South by rooting out pockets of diehard secessionists—an assignment that had cost him his life. Where the Remingtons were concerned, the fruit had not fallen far from the tree.

"It's the United States Army that needs your assistance this time," Bronson told them. "We have a grave problem on our hands and if it isn't resolved we could face a disaster here in the Southwest, with widespread desertion or outright mutiny in forts and outposts from the Brazos River west to the Guadalupe Mountains and as far south as the Rio Grande."

Cord and Emma exchanged glances. Ezariah Bronson was not prone to exaggeration. Cord knocked back his whiskey and held up the empty glass to catch the alert steward's attention. "The only thing I can think of that would have that kind of effect on army garrisons would be payroll."

Bronson nodded grimly. "Absolutely right. The payroll for the garrisons manning a string of forts in the western half of Texas in response to the Comanche threat, is transported by ship down the east coast and thence to New Orleans, and from there by rail to Fort Worth. The problem is that even though the Atchison, Topeka & Santa Fe is pushing south towards El Paso from right where we are sitting, and the Southern Pacific Railroad is heading for the same destination from the west, and the Texas & Pacific is laying track westward, it's going to be another ten years at least before garrisons in or around the Llano Estacado can be effectively provided for by rail.

"Until then, payrolls are transported by wagon from the railhead, which is currently at Wolf Creek, some forty miles southwest of Fort Worth. And three weeks ago the train traveling north from the port at Galveston, carrying over twenty-six thousand dollars, was attacked before it even got to Fort Worth. This was two months' pay for the garrisons of Forts Clark, Griffin, Stockton, Richardson, Davis, McIntosh and Phantom Hill. The shipment was waylaid. The money was taken. The train were burned. And the detachment of soldiers accompanying those wagons were slaughtered."

"That doesn't sound like the handiwork of your run-of-the-mill outlaw gang," remarked Emma.

"The Seminole scout riding with the patrol from Fort Clark that arrived on the scene a day after the robbery estimated about forty or fifty horsemen."

Cord whistled softly. "How did they stop the train?"

"Dynamited the tracks ahead of time, so the train was derailed."

"Sounds to me like they knew almost to the hour, certainly to the day, when this payroll train was going to be on that track. How many people know about the shipments, and how is the information distributed?"

"Garrison commanders are notified by dispatch and have an estimated date of arrival. And the various details assigned to protect the shipment during transport also had knowledge."

Cord nodded. Most army forts were not in areas where telegraph service was available. "But what about the railroads? Was there telegraph traffic regarding the payroll shipment?"

Bronson grimaced. "Yes. And I realize that may be how the robbers learned of the shipment's route and estimated times of arrival."

Again, Cord nodded. Splicing into telegraph lines and then using a boxed key and relay had been a tactic employed by both sides during the Civil War to intercept transmissions and produce false ones. "Did the army try to follow the trail of these robbers?"

"They sent the Seminole. The trail took him north to the Red River. Apparently, the robbers crossed into Indian Territory. We believe they have their base in Cherokee country. The Cherokees will not welcome a federal force on their land, for several reasons."

"Who can blame them," said Cord. There was no love lost in the Cherokee Nation for the United States. The Cherokees had been forced to leave their ancestral homeland by President Andrew Jackson forty years ago, embarking on the Trail of Tears to the land set aside for them in the Indian Territory. During the Civil War, many Cherokees had fought for the Confederacy, among them Stand Watie, who had held the rank of general.

Emma sipped her Sazerac and stopped perusing Raine, who stood at ease nearby, to turn her sea-green eyes on Bronson. "So what would you like us to do? Find these robbers and get the army's money back?"

"That would be nice, my dear. But the top priority is to protect another shipment that will be sent out from Baltimore in a week or two. That shipment should arrive at Wolf Creek, under guard, in about a month. It will include pay for the garrisons of Forts Griffin, Richardson, Concho and McKavett as well as the outposts at Camp Wichita and Mountain Pass. I would like for you two to be there to meet it. Do what you must to make sure it doesn't fall into the wrong hands. Furthermore, you are commissioned to find out who carried out the first robbery and bring them to justice."

"All fifty of them?" asked Cord, with a wry smile.

Bronson produced a brown packet from the inside pocket of his rumpled uniform coat, slid it across the table. "The letters contained therein, signed by President Ulysses S. Grant himself, will secure you the services of all military personnel, including the Quartermaster General at the depot in Fort Worth and every commanding officer in the forts along the Texas frontier. I expect you to be diplomatic with regard to the power these give you when it comes to dealing with private citizens."

While Cord opened the packet, perusing the letters it contained, Emma finished her drink and asked, "How many soldiers were in the detail trying to protect the first shipment?"

"Sixteen, commanded by a lieutenant who was a veteran of the war. And sixteen bodies were recovered. Many were burned beyond recognition."

"No idea who might be leading this—well, it sounds more like a paramilitary force than a gang of highwaymen," said Cord.

Bronson leaned forward, elbows on the table, hands clasped tightly together. "No idea. But not just any man can keep forty or fifty hardcases in line, or plan and carry out a robbery like that. Find out who that man is and kill or capture him, and I would wager that will go a long way to resolving our problem."

Raine stepped forward to remove Emma's empty glass, but when he reached for it she grabbed his hand and turned it slightly, examining it.

"You have such big, strong hands," she murmured, with admiration. "Do you carry the Smith & Wesson Schofield?," she said.

"No, miss, still got this," said Raine, reaching under his fatigue blouse and brandishing the 1860 Colt Army he carried under his belt at the small of his back. He offered it to her, grip first.

Bronson was startled. "Cletus, why on earth are you carrying a pistol when the Remingtons are here?"

"My orders are to keep you alive, Colonel," said Raines. "Cain't take no chances." He glanced apologetically at Emma and Cord. "No offense."

"None taken," said Cord.

Emma studied the pistol and shook her head. "The Schofield will fit your hand much better than this. Cord and I both carry one—well, actually, I carry two. Fires cartridges. These old cap-and-ball *pistolas* will get you killed these days. The trigger guard is larger, and the trigger itself is recessed. I'm surprised you don't have one. The army began issuing them a few years ago."

"Ninth Cavalry, Miss. We be the last to get everything."

Emma glanced at Bronson, eyebrow raised. The Colonel was staring at her. Emma's smile and the gleam in her eye when she looked at Raine, along with the way his aide was staring raptly at her, made him wonder if they had been intimate at some point in the past. This wasn't the first time he had met with the Remingtons to discuss a job, and Raine had been with him for many years. He had tried to ignore the looks that passed between them before, but he could do so no longer. Emma was a free spirit who flaunted her sexuality, refusing to be subdued by the morals of the age. There were a few others like her – Victoria Woodhull and Fanny Wright came to mind – but she was the one undressing his aide with her eyes.

"Really, Emma," he said somberly. "I would prefer you didn't flirt with my aide, especially when we are discussing business."

"My apologies, Colonel," she said, sounding contrite. But Bronson thought he detected a wry curl on her lips. Emma's gaze returned to Corporal Raine. "I will get you a Schofield," she promised, and handed the Army Colt back to him, throwing in a brazen little smile for good measure. Then she glanced at her brother, hands on hips, as though he was the one holding things up. "Are we ready?"

"Oh yes," said Cord, amused. "We're ready." He rose and shook hands with Bronson. "We'll leave first thing in the morning, Colonel."

"You will both be well-compensated, as always. And you two are welcome to accompany me back to Fort Leavenworth, and from there travel by rail south and then west to Fort Worth." He glanced dubiously at Emma and Raine once more.

"Thank you, Colonel, but we'll go by horseback," replied Cord. "We have well-conditioned mounts, and can make fifty, sixty miles a day. Ten to twelve days will see us to the railhead. Switching from one railroad to another half a dozen times, it would take us a fortnight at least to get from here to there."

"Straight across the Llano Estacado, then," said Bronson. "Lot of people have gotten killed out there. Be careful."

"We will do our best not to add to the carnage," drawled Emma.

III.

The first indication that Cord and Emma received that they weren't alone on the Staked Plains was the low-pitched waffling buzz of a bullet that passed to the left of them. As Cord whipped his tall bay horse around he wasn't surprised that his instincts had been true, that they HAD been followed. Far off to the northwest he could just make out horsemen—three of them—about five hundred yards away, a quarter of a mile. He knew from the distance involved that the shooter had a buffalo rifle. Even a Springfield rifle was only accurate to about a hundred and fifty yards. "Ride!" he shouted, as the bay responded to being reined around in a complete circle. Emma was already in a gallop, bent low over the roan's neck, shouting at her brother to "Come on!" He kicked the bay into a leaping gallop and steered the horse into Emma's dust, towing the packhorse.

Cord had been blessed with the ability to keep his head while under duress, and in a mere moment had calculated the odds, eliminated unworkable solutions, and chosen a tactic that provided the best chance of survival. He urged the bay to longer strides and came up alongside his sister as several more bullets buzzed angrily past them.

"Give me the reins!" he shouted, above the thunder of shod hooves on hard-packed dirt and the loud huffing exhalations of horses at full gallop. "I'll decoy. You hole up!"

Emma didn't hesitate. She knew it was inevitable that one of them or one of their horses would soon be struck if they simply tried to outrun their pursuers. Handing her reins to her brother, she pulled her Winchester '73 out of its saddle boot and drew her booted feet back until just her toes were pressing into the stirrups. Cord moved in front of her, leading her roan now, and she narrowed her eyes and clamped her lips tight against a cloud of dust. She couldn't see much, and had to trust that Cord would give the signal at just the right time. Her spine crawled as her body anticipated the impact of a bullet.

Cord didn't ride in a straight line, but swung the roan left and right in long tight arcs. He knew this allowed their pursuers to close the distance, but he didn't plan on running for long. He stayed low and kept his eyes peeled and soon enough saw what he was looking for, a line of brush punctuated by a few wind-twisted mesquites that curled across the semi-arid plain a hundred yards ahead, indicating that standing water was sometimes present there. He made a bee-line for it, slowing the bay into a lope as he shouted "Go!"

Emma swung her left leg up and over the roan's neck and slid out of the saddle, trying to land on the run. She lost her balance and fell, turning her body so that she rolled on a shoulder as she hit the ground. The impact knocked the wind out of her, but she was up and running nonetheless, sprinting into the cloud of dust, catching a glimpse of her brother kicking the bay into a gallop and a heartbeat later leaping over the narrow gully, marked by the serpentine line of brush and trees. Her roan followed suit. A bullet buzzed close by and she saw a spurt of dust in front of her and to the right. Coming to the rim of a steep, sandy, five-foot embankment, she slid down it. Staying low for a moment, catching her breath, she levered a 44.40 cartridge into the chamber.

Her rifle was a One of One Thousand which she had purchased for one hundred dollars in Santa Fe a fortnight before Ezariah Bronson's visit. Having spent quite a few rounds acquainting herself with her new acquisition, she was convinced that it was indeed even more accurate than the standard Winchester '73.

Raising her head up over the rim, fairly sure that her dismount had been concealed by the dust, Emma glimpsed the three riders, now no more than three hundred yards away. They were shooting at Cord—she heard the bullets passing overhead—which inclined her to believe they weren't aware she had dismounted and was waiting for them. Cord's strategy had worked and she didn't question whether it was the one that gave them the best chance to prevail. Had she and her brother turned to fight the moment they had been fired upon, those three would have hunkered down and used their longer-range buffalo rifles to full advantage, killing their horses first. Then they would have all the time in the world to kill their prey.

She ducked down below the rim of the embankment and glanced up and down the gully. It was no more than six feet wide and in some places even more narrow. She crossed the gully, leaned her back against the southern embankment and concentrated on her breathing, drawing air slowly into her lungs and exhaling through pursed lips while she listened to the thunder of hooves, gauging the distance between her and her targets solely on the volume of that sound. It was only a matter of seconds before the pursuers reached the gully, but time had slowed down for Emma. Her pulse was slow, her mind clear. She brought the crescent butt plate of the Winchester to her right shoulder as the first two pursuers to reach the gully jumped it to her left. When the first rider appeared, a little to her right, she squeezed off a shot just as the man's horse launched itself into its leap. She caught a glimpse of a burly, bearded rider clad in buckskins and a Kossuth hat. The bullet struck him squarely in the chest and knocked him backwards out of the saddle. He landed on the rim of the opposite embankment but she wasn't paying him any attention by the time that happened. She knew he was dead.

Wasting no time, she scrambled up the southern embankment. One of the other two pursuers had checked his horse and was reining it around. The other was apparently unaware that a companion had been lost and was riding on, keeping after Cord, and getting off one more shot. Emma brought the Winchester to shoulder and fired, not once but twice, the reports one second apart. The nearest man threw his arms up and toppled over the back of his spinning horse. The third man slumped forward and then slid sideways out of the saddle. The riderless horses ran off in different directions.

She walked closer to the last two men she had killed. It wasn't to make sure they were dead. She already knew that to be the case. But she was curious to know who they were. It seemed likely they were buffalo hunters, considering their appearance. In the old days, when bison were plentiful, they were killed sometimes just for the tongue and skinning was at best haphazardly performed, with many skins ruined by poor shooting or ignorance of the way to properly cure one. But now the herds had dwindled in size, and the last of any consequence roamed the Llano Estacado With the Comanche threat largely eliminated, more and more buffalo hunters were being seen in Texas. Most worked in small groups now, with each member of the group specializing in some aspect of the trade. There might be one or two shooters, one or two skinners, and someone who could both cook and knew how to stretch hide.

A single gunshot rang out to the south. A pistol. She hurried out of the brush and stopped dead in her tracks. Cord was standing about a hundred yards away, a pistol in one hand, the bay's reins in the other. And her roan lay still on the ground.

"No," she breathed, and then began to run. "No ... no ... NO!"

Seeing her coming, Cord strode forward to intercept her, leading the bay. She tried to get past him but he wrapped an arm around her waist and reeled her in. "He's dead, Emma. I'm sorry. Got hit in the leg. Shattered bone. I couldn't leave him to suffer even a moment."

She dropped the Winchester and used both hands trying to push away from him, tears streaming down her dusty cheeks. "Let me go! Damn you, let me GO!"

He shook his head, and held her fast for a moment, until her crying lessened, thinking back through the events of the last few minutes, wondering if Emma's horse would have survived had they just hunkered down in the gully. His conclusion was that it may have but they probably wouldn't have. He didn't waste time trying to figure out why the hide hunters had trailed and then attacked them. The Llano Estacado was a lawless place. They could have had robbery in mind. Or rape, if they had realized that Emma was a woman. Cord was certain of one thing, though. If they had not killed the hide hunters, he and his sister would have been the ones lying dead.

"That was my job," said Emma, eventually, wiping at her eyes. "I should have done it." She pulled away from him and he let her go.

"I'll see if I can't catch up one of their horses," he said, and turned to the bay, untying the lead rope on the pack horse and leaving it in his sister's keeping. Emma riding the packhorse was a last resort—they needed what was left of the supplies as they were still two or three days shy of their destination. He vaulted into the bay's saddle without touching foot to stirrup, and rode off to leave her alone for a moment with her dead horse.

When he returned, towing a sorrel mare, she was sitting on the ground next to the roan's carcass. He stripped the old hull and blanket off the sorrel's back and went to the roan and retrieved the monogrammed black leather saddle that had been custom-made for his sister by the best saddle maker in Santa Fe. He also took the blanket beneath it, the empty rifle boot and the saddlebags in which Emma carried a few personal items. When he had her rig set up on the sorrel he turned to see her coming towards him. She had retrieved her One of One Thousand.

"She's seen better days," Cord said, referring to the mare, "But she'll get you to Wolf Creek and we'll find you better, even if we have to go on to Fort Worth to do it."

Dismal and silent in her grief, Emma just mounted the sorrel and kicked it into motion. Cord went to the bay and climbed aboard and caught up with her. He didn't say anything. There wasn't anything he *could* say to make his sister feel better. She'd had the roan for years, since her days as a trick rider in fairs and parades. He worried that they might not find a horse that could equal it. So he rode quietly by her side. Knowing Emma as he did, he felt sorry for the first stranger they met.

CHAPTER TWO

Wolf Creek

I.

The first stranger was Ned Bohannon, whose stable was on the western fringe of the town called Wolf Creek. Once through a hinged mesquite pole gate set into a low sandstone wall, the Remingtons spotted him sitting on a three-legged stool mending tack in the striped shade of a ramada. Behind him was a corral with a few horses standing in the sparse shade of a live oak, and off to one side of this was a row of roofed stalls, where a tall slender boy of about fifteen years was tending to a half-dozen horses. The boy looked around and grinned, waving at them, then went about his chores.

They had put the Llano Estacado behind them the day before, and since then had passed through the rolling, rocky, tree-strewn hills marking the western edge of the North Central Plains. They had seen small herds of cattle and some farm houses scattered along the creek for which the town had been named. Wolf Creek was on the edge of the Texas frontier.

When Cord and Emma got close, Bohannon squinted up at them, then spat a stream of brown tobacco juice off to the side and said, "Howdy. Seen y'all comin' from the west. Don't get too many people ride in from that direction. Maybe a patrol of blue-bellies or a passel of hide hunters once in a while, though these days most hunters head up north a ways, where there's a big camp called The Flats."

As he spoke, he watched Emma, who immediately dismounted and began stripping her gear off the sorrel mare, dropping it on the hardpack. When done she smacked the horse on the hindquarters. The sorrel snorted and ran off a ways, then turned and watched her.

"You aim on boardin' that animal it'll cost you fifty cent a day. That includes feed and water."

"Not my horse," she replied. "I borrowed it. You can have it."

"Have it?" Bohannon squinted suspiciously at the sorrel. "What's wrong with it?"

"It's got no spirit."

"No spirit." Bohannon mulled that over.

"No gumption," interjected Cord. "No guts. No courage. No savvy. And, worst of all, where my sister is concerned, no personality."

"Just like a woman to want a horse with personality," said Bohannon, snidely.

"Also, it's a mare," said Emma. "And mares are usually more trouble than they're worth, in my opinion. So she's all yours. Maybe you can sell it to some tenderfoot cowboy trying to make his string."

"Well that 'splains it," Bohannon drawled. "Ask me, females, be they the two-legged or the four-legged kind, are nothin' but trouble." He smirked, as though it amused him that Emma thought she should even have an opinion, being a woman.

Cord glanced at Emma, saw the glitter in her eyes, and inserted himself between her and the stable owner. "My name is Cord Remington, sir," he said, putting out a hand, "This is my sister, Emma. And you are....?"

Bohannon was a stocky man, a little on the short side, with a long, sandy-red beard and beady brown eyes, one of them turned. He wiped his grimy paw on his grimy coveralls and shook Cord's hand. "Ned Bohannon. I own this place. That's my boy, Win, over yonder. Where you from? What brings you to Wolf Creek?"

"We're from Santa Fe. And we're here on business."

The stable owner eyed them up and down, taking note of Cord's twin bone-handled Arkansas Toothpicks, one on each hip, and the Smith & Wesson Schofield in a belt holster riding on the front of his right hip—he couldn't see the twin bone-handled knives sheathed further back under the long coat—and of Emma's cross-draw rig sporting the same make of pistol. Then he admired the Winchester One of One Thousand riding in its saddle boot. "Don't surprise me none. Nobody crosses the Staked Plains for pleasure. I'd take you for bounty hunters, though I ain't never seen no woman bounty hunter before—or any woman wearing pants." He clearly did not approve.

Cord glanced again at Emma, whose eyes were hooded, her lips compressed. His sister had a short fuse and even he did not want to be in the same county if she lost her temper. He quickly brandished a tightly rolled piece of quality vellum from a pocket inside his leather coat, unrolled it and showed it to Bohannon. The stable owner leaned forward, squinting—and then his eyes widened with surprise.

"Signed by President Ulysses S. Grant himself! Well, I'll be damned."

"No doubt," said Emma, mordantly.

"Heard tell of a large gang of outlaws hereabouts?" asked Cord. "Say anywhere from thirty to fifty men."

"This is about that army payroll that got stole south of here couple months back, ain't it? Nope, never heard of a gang that big. Sounds more like a private army to me. Back fifteen, twenty years ago, there were them Comancheros up in a place called Helltown. They sometimes rode in bunches that big if not bigger. Had to, I reckon, on account of dealing with the Comanch' the way they did. But the Texas Rangers pretty much cleaned out them vermin about ten years ago."

"You have a town marshal here?"

"That we do. Name of John Mackey." Bohannon squinted at the sun, which was an hour or so shy of setting. "The jail is on Front Street, about halfway to the Alamo Freight yard on the other side of town. If he ain't there he's likely making his rounds."

Cord paid the stable owner two dollars for the boarding of his bay and the pack horse, stating he would be back soon to deal with what was left of the supplies carried by the latter. Bohannon summoned his son with a holler. Win came running up flashing a big smile at Cord and then stared wide-eyed and slack-jawed at Emma as the latter was securing her bedroll to her brother's saddle.

"Stop your gawkin' and tend to this feller's horse. Then catch up that sorrel and put her in the pen."

"Yes, Pa," said Win. Taking up the bay's reins and turning towards the stalls he looked back at Emma and gushed, "You sure are a pretty, miss!" Red-cheeked, he broke into a run, the sorrel trotting along behind.

Leaving the stable, Cord carried his sister's fancy rig slung on his back and his Spencer repeating rifle in hand, while Emma walked alongside with their saddlebags and her booted Winchester. About twenty yards to the east the road crossed a bridge barely wide enough for a wagon and then became Front Street. The bridge spanned Wolf Creek, from which the town had derived its name. Cord would discover later that Wolf Creek ran westward from its source, the Colorado River, passing to the south of town, then turning north a short distance before heading west again. It was this northern leg of the creek that the bridge spanned.

Beyond the bridge Front Street began, a wide stretch of hardpack about five- or six hundred feet long. At the first cross street, Milam, he looked left and right, trying to gauge the size and scope of the town. Milam seemed to extend a block either way.

"A smaller town than I expected," remarked Cord. "I'd say maybe two hundred people live here."

"As long as I can find a bed and a hot bath," replied Emma.

From what Cord could see, Wolf Creek, though small, was booming. Becoming the railhead on an iron road tended to do that to a town. There were people on the boardwalks, wagons and riders on the streets, and a couple of new buildings going up. The streets were raucous with sound—the hammers and saws at the construction sites, the rattle and squeak of passing wagons, the thunder of hooves as riders went by, a train whistle from the north end of town where the Texas & Pacific tracks had been laid, the tinny sounds of a piano from The Palace Saloon in the middle of town, and the various and sundry chatter, laughter and shouts of men, women and children who were out and about. Some were curious about the Remingtons, obvious newcomers whose dusty and disheveled appearance indicated they had traveled a long way.

Emma spotted a two-story establishment across the street called the Longhorn Hotel, at the intersection of Front Street with Crockett, and directly across the latter from The Palace. She changed directions abruptly and headed straight for it, with Cord following. Inside the small lobby, Cord unburdened himself, putting the saddle down as he reached the registration desk, behind which stood a small cabinet with eight slots above a single shelf which bore a large ledger. He was about to pick up a bell that stood next to an inkwell and pen when a door opened and a woman of about thirty years emerged, her lush lips curling into a welcoming smile. Emma noted that she wore a somewhat out of fashion full skirt and guessed its fullness was maintained by a crinoline petticoat rather than a bustle. Her bodice was tight and form-fitting, designed to show off her voluptuous figure.

"Welcome to the Longhorn, sir...and lady," she said, with a British accent that Cord's practiced ear identified as West Country, due to the rhoticity of the "r" in Sir. "Come for a room, have you?"

"Two rooms, actually," replied Cord. "I'm Cord Remington, and this is my sister, Emma."

"And I am Annie Pritchard, proprietor. Very pleased to make your acquaintance." She transferred the ledger to from shelf to desk and opened it. "I happen to have two rooms at the front upstairs. A splendid view of Front Street. How long will you be staying?"

"We're not sure," said Emma, as Cord, having signed the ledger, handed the pen to her. She smiled wryly, as it was obvious that the British expatriate was quite interested in her brother. This wasn't at all unusual. Cord was a handsome fellow, if she did say so herself.

"Oh marvelous!" exclaimed Annie. "I will bring a fresh pitcher of water and a clean towel every morning shortly after daybreak, and can leave them outside the door if you wish."

"Yes, please," said Emma. "I fervently hope not to be awake shortly after daybreak, or even two hours after."

Cord was perusing the signatures of people who had signed the ledger before him. He looked up at Annie, smiling warmly. "You seem to be doing a brisk trade, Mrs. Pritchard."

"Miss, please. And yes, thanks to the Texas & Pacific, my fortunes have turned." She took a key from two of the slots in the cabinet. "Come. I will show you to your rooms."

"There's no need to bother," Cord assured her.

"It's no bother! Please, follow me."

As they headed up the stairs, Cord once again toting the black saddle, Emma asked where one might go to have a bath in Wolf Creek.

"Out the door and turn left, then 'round the corner onto Crockett, and the next building down," replied Annie. "Run by a nice Chinese fellow by the name of Wong Li. He worked for the T&P for a spell and before that the Central Pacific, I believe, which as you probably know became part of the transcontinental Pacific Railroad."

Once upstairs, Cord noticed a ladder secured to a wall, and in the ceiling a hinged hatch.

"My business partner's idea," said Annie. "He told me that back east some businesses with upper floors were putting in roof hatches, in case a fire broke out and it was impossible to get to the first floor."

Annie unlocked Emma's door first. She went in first to open the drapes on the single window, smooth out the patchwork quilt on the four-poster bed, and peek into the water jar. "Enjoy your stay, Miss Remington," she said warmly, handing over the room key.

Emma thanked her, and as Annie left the room, smirked at Cord while he brought the saddle in and set it down at the foot of the bed. "Are we going straight to the jailhouse or shall I take a nice hot bath while you are, um, otherwise occupied?"

Cord chuckled. "We'll be going to find the marshal in a moment," and left the room, closing the door behind him.

Annie performed the same routine with the window, bedcover and water jug in Cord's room, and then lingered, hands behind her back, and smiled brightly at him. "Is there anything else you might have need of, Mr. Remington?"

"I do have a question, Miss Pritchard. Do you happen have a guest currently who has been in town for a few weeks, or longer?"

"What a curious question, Mr. Remington." She paused, expecting elaboration, but when Cord just smiled and nodded and said nothing more, clearly awaiting her reply, she said, "The majority of my trade are men employed by the T&P, or men who have come with business for or with the railroad. About a week ago a peddler of potions stayed two nights. Then there was the gambler, who stayed a few nights, but then he got a free room at the jail. Seems he got angry with a percentage girl at the Palace and punched her. That's something you might get away with behind closed doors, but in a saloon full of other men, it was, let's say, foolhardy."

Cord nodded agreement. "Thank you, Miss. Is this the only hotel in Wolf Creek?"

"Yes, but there is a boarding house, run by a widow named Brewster. You can find it out on Muleshoe Road. And please, call me Annie." She stepped closer, brushed at the dust on the lapel of his leather coat. "It appears you have come a long way across hard country. I would be happy to, um, wash and clean your clothes for you, if you like."

"I might take you up on that ... later. Right now, though, I need to find your town marshal."

Annie smiling pensively. "Since it seems you might be in town for a while, I suppose I should tell you. According to the local gossip mongers, I fled my homeland and ended up here in Texas to escape the consequences of a scandal involving … let's just say he was a famous member of the aristocracy. While in Galveston I met this gentleman from Baltimore who was looking for a fresh start himself, and together we traveled here, where he built this hotel. Shortly after its completion, he took a ride one day and was never seen or heard from again. To my surprise, he left the hotel to me in his will. So you can well imagine the kind of rumors floating around about me." She shrugged. "I just hope you won't think poorly of me should they reach your ears."

"There will always be rumor and innuendo when you are a beautiful woman, Annie."

She was startled. "Do you mean that?"

"You mean about rumor and innuendo?" he asked, ingenuously.

She laughed softly. "No, the other part!"

Cord smiled. "I do indeed. Now, if you will excuse me, I need to go tend to some business."

She took his hand and turned it palm up and put the room key in it. At the door she turned to ask, "What kind of business are you in, Mr. Remington?"

"I am … a problem solver."

A few moments later, as he and Emma left The Longhorn and headed for the Jail, a stone's throw to the east and on the north side of Front Street, Emma remarked, "It seems Annie Pritchard is quite taken with you."

"I like her, enjoyed talking with her. She's intelligent, well-spoken, and has a sense of humor."

"Oh? Does that mean you will be leaving your door unlocked at night?"

"Now, now. Do I pry into your personal affairs? No I do not. I mean, I can't even keep track of them."

Emma huffed, feigning indignation, then punched him playfully in the shoulder.

II.

Entering the jail, they saw a gray-haired man sitting in a sturdy cane chair behind a scarred-up kneehole desk in the small front room, idly twirling his bushy mustache as he read from Thomas Hardy's *Far from the Madding Crowd*. The rest of the room was barely large enough for a narrow army-issue cot and a potbelly stove containing a small, lively fire that kept the interior warm. The man had his booted feet propped up on a cluttered desk. There was a five-pointed star pinned to the lapel of his black coat. His steely gray eyes rose to latch onto the Remingtons as they came in.

"Afternoon, folks. I'm John Mackey, town marshal. What can I do for you?"

"Good book," remarked Cord, with a friendly smile. "Looks like the first American edition if I'm not mistaken." Closing the door and moving nearer the desk, he studied the novel's cloth cover more closely. "Yes. Henry Holt of New York."

"That's right," said Mackey, pleased and surprised. "My ma taught me to read, but I never had much chance to do it, growing up on a farm, then fighting in the war, and then trying to ply my trade as a lawman in places like Wichita and Waco. Now that it appears I'll be spending the autumn of my life in this little town, I've been ordering books from a bookseller in New Orleans by the name of Othello Marvais."

"I know Othello!" said Cord. "I had the good fortune to visit his shop once. He has an amazing collection of antique books going back to the 17th and 18th centuries. So what do you think of Hardy's newest novel?"

Emma smiled patiently. It was just like Cord to be enthused and loquacious when he met a fellow bibliophile. Her brother spent much of his spare time reading anything he could get his hands on. His mind was like a sponge, soaking up everything he read. She wandered over to the stove and warmed herself a moment. As the day began to wane the temperature was dropping, and the night promised to be quite cold. There was a blackened pot on top of the stove, containing coffee that smelled like it had been cooking all day. After a moment, she strolled over to a heavy timbered door reinforced with iron bars. She assumed it to be the door to the jail's cellblock. She tried the door latch and found it to be unlocked. As usual, acting like she owned the place, she swung the heavy door open and looked inside. There were two cells on either side. In the rear wall was a door that was both barred and padlocked. She assumed it led to an alley. Three of the cells were empty. The appearance of the man sitting on the bunk in the fourth cell startled her He was a lanky, scrawny man with ragged clothes that he might have stolen off a scarecrow. He had wildly unkempt hair and a scraggly beard and he stared at Emma with big, startled eyes.

"I'm liking it," said Mackey, speaking to Cord but watching Emma once she opened the cellblock door. "Curious to see which of Bathsheba Everdene's suitors wins her hand. I suppose I'm partial to Gabriel Oak, even though she has just rejected him."

Cord nodded, remembering the details of the novel as though he had read it yesterday. "The middle-aged landowner, Mr. Boldwood, was the smart choice for her, I suppose. I thought it would be Troy, the dashing army sergeant, considering her nature. But Oak was the only one of the three who seemed more interested in Bathsheba's happiness than his own."

Mackey held up a hand, chuckling. "Don't spill the beans and tell me which one she chooses."

"I wouldn't do that to you, Marshal."

Emma had come out of the cell block, closing the door. "You have a prisoner. Who is he?"

Mackey looked from her to Cord, his curiosity piqued. Taking his feet off the desk he leaned forward in the chair. "His name is Willie. And who might you be, Miss?"

"I'm Emma Remington. This is my brother Cord."

"We're here on behalf of the United States government," said Cord, and produced the vellum letter he had shown Ned Bohannon earlier.

Mackey read every word contained in the document, then rolled it up and returned it to Cord and sighed. "I'll hazard a guess that your presence here means there's another payroll shipment rolling in soon. As you probably already know, I am not kept informed about such matters."

Cord considered telling Mackey that the next shipment would likely arrive in a matter of days. But then he remembered Emma's question, and joined his sister at the doorway to peer in at the man, sitting on the bunk in one of the cells, staring at his sister's back.

Mackey stood up, went to the stove to pour a cup of coffee in a tin cup, grabbed a ring of skeleton keys from a peg on the wall, then came up to the cell block door. The Remingtons made room for him to pass. The marshal unlocked the cell and went in to hand the prisoner the cup. Then he took a blanket off the bunk, shook it out, and draped it around the scrawny man's shoulders.

"His name's Willie," said Mackey. "Or so he says. No one knows anything about him or has bothered to find out. He's been here going on a month now, and you could say he's Wolf Creek's town drunk. Seems every town has to have one. Don't know where he come from, either. He was first seen shuffling down the road from the east. When someone asks him what his name was, where he came from, what kind of work he's done, his usual answer is 'Don't know, don't care.'

"Most folks here just ignore him. Some give him charity, Like Amos Chelico, the owner of the Continental, will give him a plate of food every day, though he has to eat it behind the restaurant on account of how ripe he smells. Somehow he seems to come up with enough coin to buy a bottle of cheap rotgut every now and then. And when the night is going to get cold he comes here and I let him sleep in a cell."

"Why do you lock the door?" asked Emma.

"He asked me to." Mackey shrugged. "Maybe it makes him feel safe. But it suits me so I do it." He stepped out of the cell, locked the cell door, and went out to the front room.

Cord and Emma followed him. "Did any other stranger come to Wolf Creek in the past couple of months and end up staying?" asked Cord, settling his long frame in a chair facing the desk.

Mackey thought about that a moment. "Sodbuster name of Graham came in with his family, staked a claim out along Rockbottom Road. Has a wife and a passel of kids, four I think. I haven't seen him but once, when he came to town for supplies. Which reminds me. There's John Smith, the owner of the general store. He was a drifter, I think, and just happened to sit down at a poker game and won the store." He peered at Cord. "Why do you ask?"

"I don't think the men who robbed that payroll shipment south of Fort Worth are your run-of-the-mill owlhoots. They knew where and they knew when, and by when I mean to the hour, because they knew when to blow the rails so that the next train, the one carrying the payroll, was the one derailed. Another train passed that point earlier that day, going north. So these robbers had information they shouldn't have had. They either stole that information, maybe by cutting into a telegraph line, or bought that information with a bribe. Or they may have spies."

"And there's no reason to believe they'll be satisfied with just the one haul," added Emma, who had moved to the office's only window to gaze out at the hustle and bustle on Front Street. "Regardless of the crime, most criminals won't stop until they're caught or killed."

"I see where this is going, now," said Mackey, worrying his bristly mustache with fore and middle finger. "If this gang has a spy or two, then what better place than Wolf Creek, the end of the Texas & Pacific Railroad, where the payroll will await the arrival of a wagon detail from Fort Griffin."

Rising from the chair, Cord said, "Thank you for the information, Marshal. I know we can count on you to keep our identities and reason for being here to yourself." He extended a hand across the desk.

Mackey rose to shake the hand and then looked pensively past Emma and out the window. "You know, I liked this town better when we didn't have a railroad running through. Twenty years ago I was a young deputy down San Antone way, spoiling for a fight so I could prove my worth." He shook his head, smiling pensively. "I was young and foolish back then, and damn lucky, to boot. But I'm no spring chicken now, and I don't go looking for trouble anymore."

"Leave that to us," said Emma cheerfully. "If you see or hear of anything suspicious, let us know. We're staying at the Longhorn."

III.

Less than an hour later, as the last streaks of daylight leaked out of the darkening sky, Cord and Emma were luxuriating in cast iron bath tubs filled with steaming hot water in the back room of Wong Li's bathhouse, a clapboard building with a peaked roof located right behind the Longhorn. The base of the tubs were shaped like the bottom half of a barrel, while the upper part resembled the back of an armchair and as a consequence were comfortable to sit in.

After leaving the town jail, Cord had wanted to visit the Continental for that big home-cooked meal he had been dreaming of for weeks, while Emma was insistent that cleanliness came before sustenance. As usual, she won the day. Now they sat in steaming, sudsy water, separated by a well-constructed wooden divider decorated with brightly-hued Chinese dragons.

"You really think these robbers have eyes in Wolf Creek?" asked Emma.

She had soaked a while and then washed her hair and now one of Wong Li's daughters, having just applied a fragrant oil on her scalp, was brushing out her long raven tresses, while she was leaning forward, carefully using a Perret razor to scrape the hair off her legs. Wong Li, who apparently was the only member of his family that spoke English, had recommended a plaster made of gum resin on leather to remove the hair, but Emma had insisted on the razor. "Lola Montez may have been a masochist but I'm certainly not," she declared. It was left to Cord to explain to the puzzled patriarch that Lola Montez had been an Irish actress and courtesan who became the mistress of a Bavarian king. She had also been an advocate for women using plaster to remove body hair. She had been spent her last years in the United States. "Where she died of syphilis, by the way," chimed in Emma.

"Well if you were after the payroll wouldn't you want an informant in this town?" replied Cord. "And I think we have two possibilities already."

He had read a week-old issue of the *Wolf Creek Chronicler* while soaking, and then allowed Wong Li to give him a nice close shave because it was included in the price of the bath. He and Emma were well off, especially by frontier standards, but he was still parsimonious—he put it down to his Scottish roots on his mother's side—while his sister was profligate when it came to money. Now he was vigorously washing his hair to get the sand and grit of the Llano Estacado out of it.

"You suspect Willie," surmised Emma.

"Well, I don't know if 'suspect' is the right word." He plunged his head into the soapy water and came up a few seconds later to add "But the timing is right, so he's worth keeping an eye on."

"And the other?"

"John Smith, the town's new storekeeper."

"He could hardly have planned to win the store in a poker game."

"No, but he could have made sure to win the hand if the opportunity arose."

"You mean he might be a cardsharp, like you?" Emma was quite proud of her brother and his many skills. One of those was as a cardsharp, which he had first demonstrated with Three-card Monte at the fairs and festivals where they had both honed their special talents—he with knife and a "California prayer book" and she with horseback riding and firearms. Cord had mastered the art of palming cards, dealing seconds, recovering the cut and building a deck. He had used these abilities in sleight-of-hand performances to impress crowds from one end of California to the other, and was a big part of what had made the Remingtons marquee headliners at the ages of nineteen and sixteen respectively.

"Could be. Anyway, since the shipment has yet to arrive, tomorrow I'll keep an eye on Willie. You should get acquainted with Mr. Smith."

The Chinese girl had finished with Emma's hair and spoke in Chinese, touching her back while showing her a pumice stone. Emma shook her head and stood up, while Cord, hearing the girl's offer, spoke up. "Nǐ kěyǐ cāxǐ wǒ de bèibù." The delighted girl hurried round the divider, excited to find a stranger with whom she could communicate, and she began talking non-stop. Stepping out of the tub, Emma chuckled, wondering if her brother would regret learning fluent Chinese during the two years they had spent as young teens with their father, who served as a military adviser and expeditor for the Central Pacific Railroad until that day in 1869 when a golden spike joined the CPRR with the Union Pacific Railroad at Promontory Point, Utah, creating a transcontinental iron road. Twelve thousand Chinese emigrants had worked on the CPPR. Becoming aware of his penchant for picking up foreign languages, Cord had subsequently become fluent in Spanish, French, German and Russian before turning eighteen.

Emma was pensive as she stood there, using a towel to dry off, thinking back to those halcyon days of adventure and innocence spent with her father. She had last seen Silas Remington a week after the golden spike was driven, when she and Cord had been shipped home to San Francisco by train while their father headed east and then south by rail to New Orleans, on "official military business" only to die in a dark alley at the hand of person or person unknown—unknown until she and her brother had gone down there and found the bastards responsible.

A woman's shrill shout startled her and she reached for the Schofields in her cross-draw rig, which hung from a stout peg driven into the clapboard wall behind the bathtub. Then Wong Li's wife came into view, dragging one of her nearly grown sons by the air. Both mother and son looked at the slender, raven-haired and buck-naked woman aiming the pistols at them and the former shrieked, the latter grinned, and then the mother and pulled her gaping boy on by in a hurry.

"Seems you had a secret admirer peeking around a corner," said Cord, sounding amused.

Emma got dressed. Her shirt and trousers had been washed and then dried over the hot crackling fire Wong Li and his family maintained out back to heat up buckets of water which his sons carried up from the creek. Once her boots, holsters and duster were on she looked round the end of the divider at Cord, who was leaning forward, chin on arms draped across drawn up knees, while the Chinese girl chattered away as she scrubbed his back.

"Think I'll head for the Continental for supper," said Cord. "Care to join me? Mr. Smith can wait until tomorrow."

"Fine," said Emma. "I'll be out front." She started to turn away, then turned back. "This John Smith better be handsome."

"And you had better be careful. If he should be one of them, then he's a cold-blooded killer."

CHAPTER THREE

The Rusted Bucket

I.

Cord woke from a deep and restful sleep at dawn, swung his long legs out of bed and went to the window to look down at Front Street. There were still stars visible in the indigo sky, and a thread of pinkish-orange to the east. Dressing quickly, he armed himself with the Schofield revolver and his pair of knives, leaving the Spencer rifle in the room. Listening a moment at Emma's door, he concluded that his sister was still asleep. Her job was to keep an eye on Wolf Creek's new storekeeper, and Cord knew exactly how she would go about it—by meeting John Smith and letting him get to know her. Odds were excellent that once he did, Smith would want her around morning, noon and night. If he didn't, that in itself would make Cord suspect that the man had something to hide.

Since it was unlikely the general store would be open for another hour or so, Cord chose not to wake his sister and left the Longhorn, shrugging on his long leather jacket to ward off the brisk cold of early morning, bending his steps east along Front until he arrived at the Continental. As he had hoped, the restaurant was open.

There was a sign just inside the restaurant instructing customers to leave their firearms at the door. The sign bore the name of the proprietor, one

Amos Chelico. Having been here the night before for supper, Cord didn't bother reading the sign again. He hung his gun belt on one of the wall pegs and took a table by the plate glass window at the front. The only other people in the place were a couple whose clothes had him thinking they were town folk. They both nodded amiably at him as he entered.

A tall, willowy girl brought him some coffee, the same girl who had waited on him and Emma the night before. Cord ordered a breakfast of steak and scrambled eggs accompanied by strong black coffee. The girl was shy and soft-spoken and had big eyes in an oval face that made it appear she was in awe of everything she saw. She was certainly gazing on him that way now. He had tried to engage her in conversation when she took his order the night before, but she had ended up red-cheeked and flustered. In the four years he and Emma had been making a living as troubleshooters, he had learned that the ability to strike up a conversation with people sometimes elicited information that helped them do their job. This morning he simply acknowledged her with a polite "Morning" and left it at that, not wishing to embarrass her again.

It wasn't Ivy who delivered his breakfast, but rather a slight, slender balding man of about fifty years, wearing an apron over his well-cut gray frock coat, complete with vest and cravat. After placing the platter loaded with food in front of Cord he extended a hand and said, with a faint Old World accent, "Good morning, Sir. My name is Amos Chelico, the proprietor of this establishment and a member of the Wolf Creek town council."

Cord took the hand and shook it. "Cord Remington. A pleasure to meet you, Mr. Chelico."

"Ivy told me this morning about a very interesting young couple who had supper here last night, and just now remarked that the man was back, so I had to come see for myself," explained Chelico, chuckling. With a perfunctory "May I?" he sat down across the table from Cord.

Taking a bite of the steak and finding it to his liking, Cord glanced up, a querulous cant to his brows. "I expect you get a lot of interesting people here now that the railroad has arrived."

"True, true. I think it was the crossdraw rig the woman you were with was wearing. And she happened to see your knives as well."

Cord opened his longcoat so that Chelico could see the pair of bone-handled blades sheathed at his side. "Still wearing those. The sign only mentioned firearms."

"Quite alright, Sir. Quite alright." The restaurant owner tilted his head curiously. "Are you by chance with the Texas & Pacific? Please, forgive me if I seem to be prying. But Ivy is clearly infatuated with you. She asked me to find out who you are."

"Did she now. How long has she been working here?"

"For years. Since she was a child, really. Her father and I became the best of friends. When he died I took her under my wing. I confess that now I think of her as my own daughter. The child I never had. I am obliged, you see, to look out for her. I hope I don't offend you, Mr. Remington."

"Not at all. And yes, I'm with the railroad. I'm a business agent." It was a story that he and Emma had agreed on during their journey across the Llano Estacado. For the sake of their "cover" she was still his sister, just along to sightsee. "My job is to talk to businessmen, ranchers, farmers, anyone who might have need to transport goods by rail. And you don't need to worry about me where Ivy is concerned." He had no interest in the waitress. She was pretty enough, but had the vulnerable look of a girl who would fall in love at the drop of a hat, and he wasn't looking for love. He enjoyed the work he did, and one of its attractions was the travel. He had been eleven years old when his mother died, and since then he had been on the move, first with his father, and then with Emma as they moved from town to town and fair after fair as entertainers. Perhaps someday, when he was older, he would find a good woman to wed, to bear his children, and to be his companion in the twilight of life. Then he would *try* to settle down.

"Remington," said Chelico. "Any connection to Remington Arms?"

"Not as far as I know. Eliphalet Remington was the son of a blacksmith from Yorkshire. My people were from further north, The Borders as it was called. I believe Eliphalet was twenty-three when he made a flintlock rifle from scratch that was so admired he started producing it."

Chelico nodded and stood up to extend a hand. "Thank you, Mr. Remington, for putting an old man's fears to bed. Enjoy your stay in Wolf Creek. Oh, and the breakfast is on the house."

II.

When he was done eating, Cord walked a block west on Front Street to the Jail. Now that the sun had risen, casting his long shadow in front of him, there were some people on the street. He hoped to find Willie still sleeping one off in one of Mackey's cells.

When he went through the front door the office empty. The cellblock door was closed, but not locked, and when Cord opened it he immediately saw the blanket-covered shape of the town drunk in the first cell on the right.

But Willie wasn't alone in the cell block. In one of the cells in the back, a lanky, red-headed man was tangled up with a woman. He and Emma had stopped in at that saloon on the way back to the Longhorn after dinner last night, to get what his sister called a 'tonic'—a shot of bourbon, since the bartender had never heard of a Sazerac. In ten minutes at the bar Cord had learned that the Palace was owned by a Colonel Edwin Buckley, who also happened to be the town mayor and who paid a local seamstress to make a bright red and yellow silk-and-satin outfit for all the girls who worked for him by plying the male customers with drinks and then taking any money they have left with more personal services in the privacy of upstairs rooms. This girl was wearing—at least partially—a bright red and yellow silk-and-satin outfit like he had seen on Buckley's percentage girls.

Cord was curious to know if she was one of the girls he had seen at The Palace last night, but he couldn't see her face, or much of her upper torso, for that matter, since her dress and petticoats had been pushed up above her waist. He *could* see a plump bare thigh, short but shapely legs flailing in the air, and a glimpse of one bare bouncing breast as the two coupled wildly on the cell's narrow bunk. The bunk was creaking loudly, as though it's bent and rusty metal frame was about to give way. The red-headed man was grunting and the saloon girl accompanied him with breathless squeals. It was quite a spectacle and even though they were doing it in the jail and apparently weren't too concerned with privacy, he decided to give them some. Despite the ruckus, Willie was snoring soundly as Cord left the cellblock, pushing the door nearly shut.

He went to the potbelly stove and poured himself a cup of coffee, which he carried over to the desk. Sitting in the marshal's chair and drinking some of the strong hot java, he admired the first edition of *Far From the Madding Crowd* and then perused an inch-thick stack of wanted posters he discovered in one of the kneehole desk's drawers. By the time he had committed all the images and information associated with them to memory, the cell block was quiet so he got up and ventured through the door.

The couple were lying side to side, the man with his back to Cord. The woman was the first to hear something, and her head popped up. Her eyes widened when she saw Cord and she whispered something to her lover that he couldn't quite make out. The young man looked around and shouted, "What the hell!" Embarrassed, he jumped up in a hurry and hopped around until he could get his pants all the way on and the suspenders onto his bare bony shoulders. The girl giggled at his clumsy, impromptu. She was sprawled limp and breathless on the bunk with her pale thighs spread wantonly wide. "Lord A'mighty, Kitty! Cover up!" He didn't wait for her to comply, reaching over to yank her dress down. He looked apologetically at Cord. "Sorry, Sir. Kitty and I were just ... well, she ain't needed at the saloon just yet and the marshal always does his morning rounds before he comes in, and so we came in to...well we were just...." He finally gave up, standing there with hands on his hips, shaking his head, disgusted with himself. "She and I been talkin' 'bout gettin' hitched soon. I mean I've only known her a month but I'm ...well, I'm in love." His cheeks were turning crimson.

"As long as you two don't do it in the street and scare the horses, I don't care," said Cord, amused. He gestured at the snoring town drunk. "You going to let him out?"

"The Marshal does that when he gets in." He glanced at Kitty. "You'd best get on to The Palace," he murmured, then emerged from the cell and came forward. "I'm Toby Jukes, by the way, Marshal Mackey's deputy."

"Cord Remington. I'll come back later when the marshal is here."

Kitty was making some adjustments to her dress, a pat here and a tug there, and messed with her curly brown hair and somehow no longer looked like she had just enjoyed a wildly passionate roll in the hay. Cord figured she'd had a lot of experience in making that sort of quick transformation. She walked out of the cell, giving him a salacious little wink and smile that Jukes couldn't see. Cord's nostrils flared as he caught the unmistakable scent of sex coming off her, not entirely masked by her cheap perfume. He felt sorry for the deputy if indeed Jukes was serious about getting married. All too often dancehall girls and soiled doves took advantage of lovesick men solely in order to improve their circumstances. Of course, Toby Jukes didn't look anything like the most eligible bachelor in Wolf Creek. All he had was his deputy's pay, which Cord guessed wasn't much more than a pittance. But this was not the day to speculate on Kitty's motives, and it really wasn't any of his business anyway.

Finishing his java, Cord went outside. With the sun on the rise, the frosty hint of winter he'd felt when emerging from the Longhorn Hotel an hour ago was gone and he was content to lean against a wall and watch Wolf Creek wake up. While so engaged, he saw two rowdy, loud-mouthed cowboys astride horses with a Double D brand roll into town from the west. They were boisterous because they wanted to be noticed. The cowboys he knew and had worked with were generally young and exuberant men who worked hard and played hard once they got their pay, all of which they tended to spend while in the nearest town, partaking of rotgut whiskey and loose women. Now and then they would get out of hand.

Then he saw her, and forgot all about the cowboys who were riding in. She was sashaying along the boardwalks on his side of Front Street, coming towards him, a true sight to behold, with all the ruffles and lace adorning her bustled dress. proud breasts bouncing wildly and unhindered beneath her revealing bodice, showing ankle in high laced shoes and an enticing glimpse of her flounced petticoat and pantaloons as she held her maroon overskirt up a bit with one hand. Her other hand held a matching parasol, closed and tilted over a mostly bare shoulder. She clearly intended to turn heads, and was succeeding magnificently.

The cowboys saw her too and one of them whooped and spun his horse around in a tight circle, doffing his hat with a cavalier sweep, revealing tousled wheat-colored hair. She flashed him a warm smile and the cowboy pretended to nearly fall off his mount in a swoon, before urging the horse on after his companion, who apparently was impervious by the young woman's charms. Cord smiled as he watched the tow-headed cowboy's antics. It didn't surprise him that the ranch hands rode on. Whiskey or beer was their first priority. After they quenched that thirst then came the gambling and, if they had any money left, the dollar poke with a friendly soiled dove would cap off a day to be remembered.

Cord pushed off the wall and started to saunter towards her. His first impression was that she was a beauty, and as he drew closer he confirmed that this was so. Alabaster skin, golden hair spilling out in a cascade of thick curls from under a feathered bowler, limpid hazel eyes and sensuous lips in an oval shaped face. She was drawing a lot of attention—admiration from the males on the street and disdain mingled with resentment from the females. She smiled at the men and didn't seem to be aware that the women even existed.

When she saw Cord her gazed locked on him, her eyes bright and her smile deepening. He stopped walking and angled nonchalantly against an upright of the covered boardwalk and openly admired her as she closed the gap between them. When she was near he touched the brim of his hat, flashed an easy smile, and said, "Good morning, Miss."

She stopped, tilted her head as her eyes swept him appraisingly from top to bottom, that saucy smile still inhabiting her lips. "Well hello there. Are you new in town?"

"Pretty much. Name's Cord Remington. What about you?"

She extended an arm, hand proffered, and he took it and bought it to his lips as she said, "Dulcey Garnet. And I've been here a while. Arrived last spring, right about when they put the railroad through, as luck would have it."

Her wry smile led Cord to believe that luck hadn't had a thing to do with her being here when the railroad—and all the men in its work crews—arrived. "Where do you come from?"

"I was born and raised in Virginia."

"You've a long way from home, Miss Garnet."

"You have no idea, Mr. Remington. And please, call me Dulcey." Her full lips curling wryly, she glanced down at her hand, and so did he, and only then did he realize he still had hold of it. He let go, and as she reclaimed it she dragged her fingertips light as feathers across his palm. "You have nice hands, you know," she observed. She turned his right hand over and saw the scars from his prize-fighting days. "You've been in a few dust-ups. I bet you know how to handle yourself."

Cord knew her for what she was—a whore. Every town of any consequence had at least one. He had known more than a few in his time, but could recall none as pretty and vivacious as Dulcey Garnet. It wasn't uncommon for such a girl to walk the boardwalks in her finery in order to drum up business, and he stood there thanking his lucky stars that he had been on Front Street when this woman decided to take her stroll.

"I bet you do, too, Dulcey." he replied.

"Why, Mr. Remington." She made quite a little show of pretending to be transgressed, but her wanton little smile could not be banished from her lips. "You're bold as brass," she said, her voice sultry and her southern accent pronounced. "So you're passing through? I hope that you will at least come visit me before you leave town. I stay in one of the little houses...." She stopped, then laughed, a sound that was both lilting and sardonic. "Shanties is perhaps a better word to describe them. It's not much but it's better than sleeping in an empty barrel in a dark alley. At least it gives one a smidgen of privacy."

"Have you slept in a barrel in an alley?" he asked.

"You would be astonished if I told you all the places I have laid my head down."

"Are you sure? Sounds like a good topic for pillow talk."

"Why Mr. Remington, I believe you are a true 'sporting' man," she said, pleased.

For a moment they stood there smiling at each other, and Cord wondered if she was as pleased as he by how natural their easy banter seemed to be. It was as though they had known each other longer than five minutes.

"So," she murmured, "If you go to the end of Front—" she half-turned and pointed down the street to the west "—and turn right on Crockett, and go to the end, and then down the hill to the creek, my shanty is the last one...."

Two gunshots, one on the heels of the other, cut her short. She jumped, then moved into him and Cord took her by the arms and did a half-turn, sheltering her from the street. At first he wasn't sure where the shots had come from. Then he saw several men bolting out of a false-front building bearing a sign that identified the establishment within as The Rusted Bucket. It was about six buildings down on his side of Front. He watched these men until he could be sure none of them were brandishing a gun, and then caught a glimpse of a man running across the street *towards* the saloon. It was Mackey in his black frock coat. Cord turned his attention to Dulcey.

"You'd better get off the street, Miss. I've got to go."

He didn't wait for a response, breaking into a lope along the boardwalks towards The Rusted Bucket. There were three horses tied up in front, and two of them he recognized as the ones that had carried the Double D cowboys into town. That alone confirmed his suspicion that the establishment was a watering hole. As he got closer Mackey saw him and threw an arm out, hand up, palm out, a gesture for him to stop. Then the town marshal entered the saloon. Cord understood—Mackey was telling him he didn't need help. Or, that it was none of his business. He slowed to a walk and when he arrived at the corner of the saloon he stopped entirely, peering through the plate glass window to survey the interior.

It was likely that John Mackey could handle whatever problem he was walking in on. Even so, Cord wasn't about to turn around and walk away. He would keep an eye on things, ready to back the marshal if more lead-slinging ensued.

Near the window stood three men, up against the side wall, having abandoned a poker game that cluttered the top of a nearby table. In the back, a saloon girl huddled near the piano, and the piano player sat still as a statue on the bench, his hands still on the keys. The barkeep stood pressed up against the back bar, and the two cowboys were on the customer side of the long counter. Both of the cowboys had pistols in hand, but they weren't aimed at anybody in particular. One had his back to the bar and was watching the others in the saloon while the second cowboy was facing the front door. That was where Mackey stood, just inside the batwings. Cord could see enough of the marshal to know that his guns remained holstered. There was a slow-moving pall of gray gunsmoke hovering up near the coffered tin ceiling.

"Who did the shooting?" asked Mackey.

"I did," said the cowboy who had turned to face the marshal. He was slender, towheaded and had a crooked smile on his gaunt face. Cord recognized him as the one who had reacted so melodramatically to the sighting of Dulcey Garnet. "All we wanted was a bottle," he said apologetically. "It's three days before we get paid, and this feller here—" he pointed at the barkeep "— has given us credit before. But he wouldn't this time so Burt and me both put a bullet in Dolly there as a kind of protest."

Cord was about to start scanning the floor for someone who might be named Dolly when he saw the cowboy gesture, using his six-shooter as a pointer, at a large, gaudily-framed oil painting hanging between the back-bar shelves. Its subject was a voluptuous and scantily-clad woman sprawled provocatively on a divan.

"Okay, boys," said Mackey calmly, "why don't you put those smoke-wagons away and let's talk this out."

"All's we want is a damn drink," said the other Double D hand. He was stocky, with a darker complexion than his saddle pard, and his tone was belligerent. "We're good for it."

The barkeep spoke up, his voice shaky. "There's a ten dollar limit on the credit. That's always been so. You know that, Marshal. They've used up all their credit already. None left for today. They knew this last time they left out of here, a couple weeks back."

"I forgot," said the yellow-haired cowboy. "Guess maybe I was a little drunk back when you told us."

Mackey moved from the entrance to the closer end of the bar, leaned on it with both hands showing, smiled at the barkeep. "Let's say I pay down their bills enough so that each one could get a drink. Would that be alright with you?"

The barkeep mulled that over. "Well, I reckon," he said. "But why would you want to do that, Marshal?"

"I reckon they're good for it. Besides, they ride for Tom Dundee, and I don't believe he would let anyone who rides for his brand shirk a debt."

"But what about the holes in Dolly?"

"If I'm not mistaken she has a few bullet holes in her already. I don't think your boss will make a fuss over two more."

The barkeep stood there a moment, arms folded, looking up at the painting, and then shrugged. "Yeah. Reckon you're right, Marshal."

Cord assumed that the Double D was a local cattle spread, so it made sense that Mackey would want to avoid any trouble with Dundee and his crew if he could do it without compromising himself or the town.

The tow-headed cowboy was grinning ear-to-ear, looking with great admiration at the town marshal. He holstered his pistol. "I'll be damned, Marshal!" He was in such a good frame of mind that he added, "Come payday I'll ride in and pay you back first thing."

Now that it seemed the danger was over, the three men near the window quickly scooped their money up from the table and filed out of the saloon. The cowboys seemed to have ruined their appetite for gambling. In back, the piano player and the saloon girl began talking in hushed tones, and then the latter started playing a tune, *Little Brown Jug* and commenced singing....

My wife and I live all alone,

In a little log hut, we called our own

She loved gin, and I loved rum

I tell you what we'd lots of fun.

Cord started to unwind, leaning against the corner of The Rusted Bucket, full of admiration for Mackey. The marshal had kept his head when others were losing theirs and had come up with a rational and workable solution to a knotty problem.

Looking back up the street to the spot where he had parted company with Dulcey Garnet, he was disappointed but not surprised that he didn't see her, but took solace in the sure and certain knowledge that he *would* see her again. He stayed tilted at the saloon corner with a smile curling the corners of his mouth, thinking about the raven-haired beauty and the fun they could have.

And then Mackey said, "You'll need to pay your fine with those wages, too."

Cord's smile froze in place and he turned his head to peer through the window again.

"What fine?" asked the stocky, surly cowboy.

"For discharging your firearms inside a place of business. Twenty dollar fine, and you'll need to spend tonight as my guests at the jail. That's the city ordinance, boys, and no way around it. Now, before you buy that drink, go on and slide your hoglegs down the bar to me why don't you."

Cord pushed away from the corner and with long strides headed for the saloon entrance, thumbing the leather loop off the hammer of the Schofield .45 on his hip. As he pushed against the saloon's batwing doors he heard the snarl of the stocky man. The trouble wasn't over. The tension inside The Rusted Bucket was palpable.

"I ain't paying no twenty dollars and I sure as hell ain't going to spend a night in jail for shooting a goddamn picture!" he barked, resentfully.

Cord stepped in, the batwings swinging on well-oiled hinges behind him. His gaze fastened on the stocky cowboy, who was bringing his pistol to bear on Mackey. The marshal was pushing away from the bar, sweeping his coat back with an arm as he reached for the pistol at his side. Making a split-second decision, Cord drew the Schofield, taking a half-step forward and making a half-turn to the left at the same time, his arm coming up to shoulder level and firing, all one fluid motion, without hesitation. His six-shooter boomed a heartbeat after Burt's, and then twice more, because Burt had fired on the move, and Cord's first bullet plunked into the bar. The next two hit the Double D cowboy, the first in the left shoulder, the second squarely in the chest.

Everything had slowed down for Cord. He saw Mackey double over, the slug hitting him like an ax handle in the midriff, knocking the wind out of him. His legs gave out and he fell forward, caromed off the bar and then hit the floor, but not before his trigger finger spasmed and he fired a single shot. The bullet furrowed into the floor, throwing up some splinters.

The percentage girl screamed. The cowboy who had shot Mackey was going down too, sprawling on his face, his still-smoking pistol skittering across the scuffed planks of the saloon floor.

Cord swung his arm to the right a few degrees, drawing a bead on the yellow-haired cowboy, who stood there with hunched shoulders and a scared expression on a face drained of color. His saddle pard was moving arms and legs in an uncoordinated way, like a turtle trying to crawl on ice, but not for long. By the time Cord got to Burt he was still. Cord worked his boot under the man and managed to flip him over. The cowboy was still alive, but barely. His eyes were wide and filled with panic. His mouth was gaping open and a wheezing sound came from his throat, then he coughed up some blood. The bullet had struck him a couple of inches north of the sternum. Cord felt a cold chill. He surmised that the .45 caliber slug had cracked a rib and both bone slivers and hot lead had ripped into at least one of the man's lungs. If both lungs were damaged he was likely going to drown in his own blood.

Catching movement out of the corner of his eye, Cord turned and saw the barkeep, who had ducked behind the mahogany when the shooting started, now reappearing to hasten to the end of the bar. He stood there looking down at Mackey, horrified. "He's bleeding...a lot!" he shouted, glancing up at Cord.

"Then stop standing there and go fetch the doctor!"

The barkeep glanced uncertainly at the bar. "I'm... not supposed to leave ...."

"Get moving!"

The barkeep broke into an ungainly run, and once outside he started yelling, "Marshal's been shot! Marshal Mackey is hurt bad!" as he hurried down the boardwalks.

"Is...is he going to die?"

Cord's bleak gaze swung to the yellow-haired cowboy, who was staring in horror at his friend while he posed the question in a shaky voice.

"Yep," said Cord, angrily. "All because of one night in jail and a twenty dollar fine." He shook his head, breaking open the Schofield and tugging three fresh cartridges from belt loops to replace the three spent shells. Holstering the pistol, He held out a hand and snapped his fingers impatiently. The slump-shouldered cowboy unbuckled his gun belt and handed it over "Don't move," he warned and brushed past the Double D man to kneel at Mackey's side.

The marshal was curled up in a fetal ball and was spilling plenty of blood onto the floor. Cord tried to pull one of Mackey's arms away from his body so that he could see more readily where the bullet had struck. But the marshal had his arms locked tightly around his middle. His sleeves were soaked with blood, and Cord's hand came away smeared with it.

"I need to look," he said.

"No!" Mackey wheezed. "No!" His voice was hoarse and wracked with pain.

Batwings banging against the door frame turned Cord's head and he saw a tall, slender gray-haired man come rushing inside. "Stand aside!" he snapped at Cord, dropping his medicine bag on the floor and kneeling beside Mackey. "How's the other one?" he snapped over his shoulder.

Cord glanced over at Burt. The cowboy was staring at the ceiling with an expression of panic frozen on his face. He had seen that sightless stare before.

"Gone," he said, and his voice sounded a little hollow, too.

A crowd had gathered in front of the saloon, lined up two deep at the big window, and a knot of them at the entrance. A commotion broke out and Toby Jukes burst through, shouldering a few people aside. When he saw that Mackey was down he froze in place.

Emma came in right behind him. Cord could tell she had come from the Longhorn. Her raven hair was mussed She wore her pale yellow shirt half-tucked into her pants, and was barefoot. She had her holsters—one draped over each shoulder, and had the Winchester One In One Thousand in hand too. That was Emma, he thought, always coming loaded for bear.

She went straight to Cord and on the way scanned the room and read her brother's expression and then looked at the dead cowboy. She didn't need anyone to relay to her the details of what had happened. She knew the story in a glance.

Toby Jukes had recovered from his shock enough to walk over to the fallen marshal. He took one look over the sawbones's shoulders and turned away quickly, white as a sheet. Seeing Cord, he walked over and Cord handed him the gun rig of the Double D cowboy who was still standing.

"The marshal was going to take them in for discharging firearms," explained Cord, then gestured at the man he had killed. "This one wasn't partial to the idea of spending a night in jail."

"What a stupid thing to die for," muttered Jukes. "The marshal looks to be in a bad way." He glanced at Cord as though hoping he would hear some reassurances regarding Mackey's chances, but none were forthcoming, so Jukes stood there a moment, at a loss what to do, until Emma suggested he take the yellow-haired cowboy into custody.

As the deputy hauled the cowboy away, Cord picked up the dead man's pistol, then took his gunbelt and searched his pockets, finding a small pouch of tobacco and some papers. He put all this on the bar and told the barkeep to take care of it until someone from the Double D came for the dead man's things. Then he said, "Never mind" and stuffed the items into a pocket of his breeches, thinking it would be wiser to hand them over to Jukes or deliver them to Tom Dundee himself. He put Burt's pistol back in the dead man's holster and slung the gunbelt over a shoulder.

Some of the spectators were working their way inside. Beyond that, Cord could just stand there, watching the doctor working on Mackey. He played the what-if game. What if he had come in just a few seconds sooner? He might have been able to shoot the cowboy before the latter got off a shot. Or his presence might have deterred the cowboy from engaging in gunplay altogether.

Emma took one look at her brother and knew what he was doing. She tugged on his sleeve. "There's nothing more you can do here," she said. "Let's go."

Cord shook his head. "I think I'll stick around for a bit. But you need to go see about John Smith. And, we better hope he's not one of those people standing outside. Tomorrow I'll be taking the cowboy I killed to the Double D ranch."

"Not without me you won't. Smith can wait a day."

Cord nodded. He knew there was little to be gained by arguing with his sister when she was dead set on something.

She gave her brother a smile and then waded through the onlookers clogging the doorway, keeping her head down. She hadn't considered the possibility that the storekeeper might be among those attracted to the scene by the gunfire. Her one and only concern was for Cord's safety.

Having used up all the bandages in his bag trying to staunch the marshal's bleeding, the doc sent someone to fetch sheets and blankets from the nearby Longhorn Hotel. One of the sheets was ripped into makeshift dressings and applied and finally the doctor was satisfied that Mackey wouldn't bleed out while being transported to his office. This was accomplished by using the blanket as a makeshift stretcher, with a man on each corner. Cord was one of these men.

The doctor's office—his name, according to a plate on the door, was Eugene Haster—was at the intersection of Milam and Front Streets. Once they had the unconscious Mackey laid out on an examination table, Haster informed Cord and the others that he was going to have to operate at once. While he escorted them out the door, Haster rattled off a list of what he would need for the surgery to a middle-aged woman who emerged from a back room.

Once outside, the sawbones took Cord by the arm while the other men moved away.

"Back in the saloon, John asked me to give you this," said Haster, and handed Cord the town marshal's badge. "The last thing he said before he passed out was that he wants you to take care of it until he gets back on his feet."

Cord stared at the badge in the palm of his hand. "Is that going to happen? Is he going to get back on his feet?"

Haster shrugged. "I will have a better idea on that come tomorrow. I need to see how much damage I can repair. He's losing too much blood."

With a grimace, Cord scanned Front Street. "He has a deputy."

"True that. But Toby Jukes is just a kid."

"There must be someone else in town capable of doing the job."

Haster shrugged again and turned away, obviously in a hurry to get back inside and begin working to save Mackey's life. "I've done what he asked me to do. The rest is up to you."

Cord noticed there were specks of blood on the tin star as he put it in the pocket of his long coat. It was John Mackey's blood.

CHAPTER FOUR

Dundee

I.

The day after the shooting, while John Mackey was still fighting for his life, Cord rented a buckboard from Ned Bohannon and hauled the body of the man he had shot and killed back to the Double D ranch. According to Johnny Lang, the tow-headed cowboy, the dead man's name was Burt Riggins.

Emma was along for the ride, and Cord was happy that she was, since he had no idea what kind of reception he would receive from Burt's employer. When it came to watching his back, he didn't know of anyone more capable of the job than his sister. Tom Dundee, or Burt's fellow cowhands, but his suspicion was that they wouldn't be happy to learn one of their own was dead. Cord had the town marshal's blood-stained badge in his pocket, but how much weight that piece of tin would carry was anyone's guess. While it was rare to find a genuine gunman in a ranch crew, most cowboys were handy enough with their hog-legs.

Johnny Lang, who had spent the night in the Wolf Creek jail, was riding the horse he'd come into town on, hands tied behind his back. His horse and Burt's were tied to the back of the buckboard. He had sworn he wouldn't try to run off if he could have his hands free. It seemed to be an embarrassment to be seen trussed up like he was by his bunkhouse mates. But Cord wouldn't budge and assured him it was for his sake. Lang had already proven he wasn't endowed with much common sense, and if he were to try to run off Emma would kill him.

It was another cool sunny day, one that turned cold and windy when the north wind caught them out in the open. It was coming on noon by the time they reached the ranch headquarters. Aside from a house shaped like a T with a porch all the way around, there was a barn, two bunk houses, a smithy, several more outbuildings and a number of corrals, most of them containing horses. A tall man emerged from the house and three men came around from the corrals to join him.

The tall man was barrel-chested, with gunmetal gray hair, a creased face and sun-faded eyes. He had seen a half-century at least but he was tough as nails. Cord figured this was the ranch owner. He and the trio of hired hands were all understandably grim when they saw the canvas-wrapped shape of a man in the back of the buckboard, and since they all recognized Burt's riderless horse the identity of the dead man was no mystery.

Dundee motioned for the others to stay back when Cord steered the buckboard closer to the ranch house and then checked the horse in the traces. The grim rancher walked around to the back of the buckboard, reaching into to pull apart the canvas enough to see Burt's face. Cord noted that Emma had her eyes fastened on the three grim-faced cowboys, with a wry little smile on her lips and her Winchester 73 held with the butt plate on the wagon's seat beside her, the barrel aimed at the sky. All she had to do was swing the One in One Thousand down until the repeater's forearm rested in the palm of her left hand and then all hell would break loose. Cord shifted sideways on the buckboard's bench so he could watch Dundee and still see the cowboys peripherally.

"What happened?" asked Dundee, his bleak gaze rising to fasten on Cord.

"I shot him." Cord warily scanned the faces of the three hired hands. One of them looked despondent, like he had lost his best friend. The other two looked angry and resentful. "That was after he gutshot John Mackey in The Rusted Bucket."

Dundee was clenching his jaw as he turned to Johnny Lang. The cowboy could have thrown a leg over and slid down off the horse with his hands bound but he hadn't because Cord hadn't told him he could. But Dundee took care of that, reaching up to grab the man's shirt and drag him down off the hull. Lang managed to get his feet planted in time for Dundee to give him a hard shake.

"What the hell were you thinking, God damn it!" growled the cattleman. "What did I tell you to do when you got to town?" He turned his glare on the other three cowboys. "What have I told all of you? You check your goddamn hog-legs at the marshal's office, that's what!"

"Sorry, Boss!" yelped Lang. "We-we was hankering for a drink so bad we just plumb forgot about the guns. Then we got told we didn't have no more credit, and all we did was put a bullet in that painting of a whore that's behind the bar, you know? That's when the marshal showed up. When he said he was aiming to take us to jail for the night, Burt got mad, I reckon, and shot him. Then that man there"—He looked apprehensively at Cord – "gunned Burt down."

Dundee let go of the tow-headed cowboy and gave Cord a long, appraising look. "What's your name?"

Cord told him. He draped the reins over the wagon's footboard and climbed down, confident that the horse in the leathers wasn't going to pull the load any more than it had to. He took a burlap sack from under the seat. The sack contained Burt and Johnny Lang's gun-rigs, along with the items he had found on the former's body after the shooting in The Rusted Bucket.

"You could have sent the body back with him," said Dundee, indicating Lang with a sideways nod.

"I killed your man so it was my responsibility to bring him home. Didn't know if you wanted him buried in the Wolf Creek bone orchard or not." He offered the bag to Dundee.

Cord had been keeping an eye on the cowboys but he turned to face the rancher as they spoke. No sooner had he finished his answer that he heard a guttural sound behind him, saw Dundee's eyes swing away from him and widen in surprise and in the same instant Emma barked "Cord!" Dundee hadn't taken the sack yet so Cord dropped it and began to turn, hands clenching into fists, the scuff of boots on hardpack warning him that at least one of the Double D cowpokes was charging him. He also knew that the only reason he didn't hear Emma's Winchester was because whoever was coming for him hadn't slapped leather.

He was halfway turned when the attacker ducked his head and barreled into him. The cowboy wasn't that big or particularly brawny but he was whipcord lean and tough as whang leather and he knocked Cord off balance. Cord made sure he took the man down with him. They kicked up a cloud of dust as they wrestled, the cowboy throwing wild punches, and then rolled under the buckboard. Cord's boot hit a wheel and the horse jumped. Emma grabbed up the reins with her left hand just in case.

The wind knocked out of him, Cord threw up an arm to deflect a wild punch. The cowboy's next swing produced only a glancing blow, and Cord answered by slamming a fist into the side of the cowboy's head. That loosened the man's grip on him and he scrambled out from under the wagon and got to his feet, wheezing as he tried to suck air into his lungs. The cowboy came crawling out after him, bounced to his feet and wiped at the side of his face. His fingers were smeared with blood, as Cord's knuckles had opened up a gash across his cheekbone.

The Double D ranch hand snarled and moved in, fists up and shoulders bunched. Even though he had fought the best pugilists west of the Mississippi and won more than his fair share of matches, Cord wasn't over-confident. The cowboy was tough as whang leather and for certain had been in his share of dust-ups. Cord dodged and weaved out of the way of his opponent's first few swings, caught his breath, then stepped in to block a roundhouse blow with his right arm while launching an uppercut with his left that snapped the cowboy's head back and sent him sprawling backwards.

The other two cowboys had been loudly egging their saddle pard on—until he went down. Cord spared them a quick glance to make sure their hands were empty and the hoglegs they wore were still holstered. His assailant was stunned, and struggled to get to his feet and find his balance.

"Stay down, Whit," snapped Dundee, who stood with arms folded and a grim expression on his face.

But the cowboy wouldn't listen. His pride wouldn't let him. He got to his feet, swaying, got his fists up, but he was dazed. Cord eluded a few more wild swings, not wishing to do any further damage to the man if he didn't have to, but got a little careless. A left hook stunned him. He stumbled sideways and nearly fell. Whit pressed the issue. The copper taste of blood in his mouth, Cord's ire was up then. "God damn it," he muttered, easily blocked another wild swing, and punched his opponent right in the face. Blood spurted from a broken nose and the cowboy went down like a poleaxed steer, out cold.

Dundee stepped in, glaring at the other two hired hands. "This is over," he rasped. "Take him to the bunkhouse. Find Lopez to set his nose. And tell the rest of the boys I will brook no more trouble. These two"—He gestured at the Remingtons—"are my guests."

The cowboys did his bidding, each taking an arm of the unconscious Whit and draping it over their shoulders so they could drag him, upright, across the hardpack. The rancher turned to Cord. "You harbor any hard feelings, I want to know now."

Cord worked his aching jaw, hawked and spit some blood and shook his head. "No hard feelings. I killed his friend. I don't fault him for what he did."

"You done right bringing Burt back here yourself. He worked for me going on two years. This was his home and we'll plant him here. If you'll cut Johnny loose I'll have him take care of Burt."

Cord drew one of his knives and cut Lang loose. While he did, Emma climbed down off the buckboard.

Dundee glared at Lang "Take Burt around to the back porch, get him down off that wagon and cover him with a blanket. Estella will clean up the body." He waited and watched until he was convinced his orders were being followed, then turned to extend a hand to Cord, who shook it.

"I've got no quarrel with you," said Dundee. "I reckon you did what needed doing when you shot Burt." He looked curiously at Emma, who was standing there watching, the Winchester racked across her shoulder. "Hello, ma'am."

"Miss, not ma'am." She nodded in Cord's direction. "I'm his sister."

Dundee nodded, gaze lingering on her a moment longer. He was accustomed to seeing women with firearms, but there was something about this one – the way she held herself and her rifle, her calm but alert demeanor during the fistfight—that made him think she was a shootist. He looked back at Cord. "Tell me about John Mackey. Will he pull through?"

"I don't know," admitted Cord, but even before he said it his expression and tone of voice gave Dundee his answer. "We'll be heading back." He walked around the buckboard and picked up the burlap sack he had dropped when Whit charged him, and brought it back to the rancher. "Burt's gun rig and the few belongings he had on him. Lang's pistol and holster are in there, too."

Dundee took possession of the sack. "Come on inside for a spell. I can offer you two some coffee and a hot meal."

Cord was cold and hungry, but that wasn't the only reason he was inclined to accept the invitation. Tom Dundee was no doubt one of the important men in these parts, and refusing someone's hospitality on the frontier could be construed as a personal slight unless there was a good reason for doing so. Besides, three hours riding a buckboard had been a painful reminder that he had a tailbone.

He glanced at Emma, who shrugged ambivalence—it was entirely up to him. "Alright then," he said and led the horse and the attached buckboard, to one of the tie rails in front of the house.

The Remingtons followed the cattleman into a long room warmed by a fire crackling cheerfully in a big stone fireplace. The floor was made of tightly-joined puncheon, with woolen rugs scattered about. Stout rafters supported the low-pitched roof. The furniture was solidly made too, with well-stuffed leather or hide upholstery. A big gun case on one wall held a wide array of weapons, from scatterguns to hunting rifles and shotguns, repeaters including an old Hall breechloader and a Sharps carbine. Cord imagined the cabinets below the rack contained ammunition and perhaps some short guns.

But the most eye-catching object in the long room was a big stuffed cougar on a tree-trunk base, posed in a lunge that had its long teeth bared and front paws raised. Cord stopped in his tracks and stared. The animal had been as long as he was tall, and must have weighed more than he did. Dundee chuckled, and walked over to the big cat.

"This is Two Toes. As you can see he lost a couple, probably to a trap. He was around when I got here, back before the war. Used to come down out of the hills across the creek from where the town now stands, and later moved out to Gunsight Ridge." Dundee stood with arms folded, looking solemnly at the stuffed animal. "Ordinarily I hold no grudge against a big cat or a wolf that might take down a calf or steer. But this one was different. He damn near ruined him. He didn't kill to survive. He killed because he liked it. He even killed a couple of my men. So I hired a professional hunter. Two Toes dragged his corpse back and dropped him right out yonder one night.

"He killed so many of my cattle I was just about ruined, so I went out after him myself. Wasn't going to risk the lives of any more of my men. If I didn't kill Two Toes then I was busted, so it came down to him or me." With brows furrowed and a faraway look in his eyes, Dundee drew a long breath, then glanced at Cord with a wintry smile. "Reckon I don't need to tell you who won.

"I did figure on dying, though But I also figured it was better to die fighting than to die one slaughtered cow at a time. When I got into the brush along Gunsight Ridge I soon realized I was the hunted, not the hunter. I could hear this ol' boy snarling now and then. Sometimes he was behind me, sometimes to my left, then to my right. He was tracking me—and, I think, taunting me. That night he came in close to my camp, but not close enough to see him in the firelight. I grabbed my rifle and walked out to the edge of the light and I could hear him moving away. Then later he would come in closer. This went on all night. I think he meant to keep me from sleeping. Not that I would have slept a wink up there anyway.

"Next morning, I found some rocks to settle down in, between the spires that mark the center of the ridge. That way he could only come at me from two directions. I counted on my horse to give me warning. All that day I waited, and didn't hear him anymore. I believe that was the longest day of my life. It was right before sundown when he came for me. But he made one mistake. He came from the east, so the sun wasn't in my eyes. When he broke cover I jumped up on the rocks so as to have the sun right behind me. I think for an instant he lost sight of me. That was long enough for me to get a shot off, just as he was lunging. When he knocked me down I passed out, hit my head hard. I woke up drenched in blood, with this beast on top of me. He was dead, and it was his blood.

"Brought him home, not for bragging rights, but to be a reminder that some things are worth dying for. And I wanted the men to see that he was dead, as lot of them were spooked by then, saying maybe Two Toes was possessed by Lucifer himself, or some such thing. I wanted to show them it was safe to go back to work." He shrugged his shoulders, shaking off the memories. "Come, sit at my table."

When Cord asked for a chance to wash up, Dundee called "Estella!" and a moment later a stout, smiling Mexican woman appeared, to whom he spoke in Spanish. She led the Remingtons to a small room with a couple of wash basins built into counters, and an open door through which they could look down a short, covered walkway to the stone-walled kitchen. Estella left him there and went out to the kitchen. Cord shrugged out of his long coat and shook the dust off it. Then he washed his neck and shoulders and face, gingerly feeling the swelling on his cheekbone, where Whit's solid left hook had landed. While he washed, Emma strolled out the door through which Estella had passed.

To her left was the back porch, and she saw Burt's corpse lying there, covered by a blanket. Lang had hitched his horse and Burt's to one of the porch uprights and was disappearing around the corner of the house, taking the buckboard back to the front as instructed. A moment later he returned, gave her a quick and wary glance, then collected the two ponies and headed across the hardpack in the direction of the other ranch buildings.

One of these she took to be a bunkhouse. A half-dozen cowboys were collected out front, and as she watched, three of them started to walk towards the house. Just then Cord emerged from the washroom, shrugging his coat back on.

"I suspect that they're just coming to lay eyes on Burt," he commented. "I don't think any of them are going to disobey their boss." He glanced at Emma. She didn't seem the least bit concerned about the motives of the three approaching cowhands. She wasn't even watching them anymore. Instead, her attention was focused on a breaking pen hard by a corral beyond the bunkhouse, where it appeared a couple of wranglers were engaged in breaking a horse.

Estella emerged from the kitchen with a wooden tray bearing a coffee pot and a pair of glazed clay cups. "*Por aquí, Señor, Señorita,*" she said with a bright smile, in passing.

Cord turned to follow her inside, but stopped and turned back when he realized Emma hadn't budged. "You coming?"

"I'm not hungry," she replied, with a bright-eyed glance over her shoulder at him, and then she was heading off across the hardpack towards the corral. It was then that he saw the horses milling around in the corral, and understood. He wondered, briefly, if any of the Double D hands would give her, the sister of the man who had shot their pard, Burt Riggins, any trouble. He hoped not, for their sake.

Not wanting to be the cause of any more strife at the Double D Ranch, Cord followed Estella back inside the big house.

II.

Emma spared the merest glance for the trio of Double D cowboys who were walking towards the big house, and while they looked at her with sullen curiosity they didn't say a word. Nor did she. Her interest was in the goings-on at the breaking pen. A cowboy was trying to stay aboard a dark bay pinto that was bucking up a storm, and didn't stay on the 'hurricane deck' for long. The pinto added a sharp flip of the hips and sent the rider flying. The cowboy managed to get to his feet and stumble to the fence as the pinto continued to fling himself around the pen, snorting and kicking up a cloud of dust. Clambering over the fence, the rider yelled at his compadre and limped stiffly towards the bunkhouse. The second man, who had been watching the short ride from the top of the fence, slid down into the pen and unfurled a lasso. Tossing the loop round the pinto's neck, he wound it around the post in the middle of the pen, moving round the pole to keep the horse circling until it had run out of rope.

By that time the rider was coming out of the bunkhouse with a rifle in hand. Emma lengthened her stride. He climbed to the top of the fence, hooking a leg over it and shouted the wrangler to stand clear. It was the wrangler who first spotted Emma.

"We got company, Will."

The man with the rifle looked around—just as Emma reached him, grabbed the back of his belt and pulled. Will fell backwards and hit the hardpack, landing on his side, a fall that knocked the wind out of him. The other man scrambled out of the pen and brushed past Emma to take a knee beside Will, who grabbed his arm, wheezing as he struggled to suck air into his lungs. The wrangler glared at Emma

"I'd beat the tar out of you if you wasn't a woman," he said, sullenly.

She ignored him, extending a hand to Will. "Come on, stop sitting in the dirt. Get up, and tell me about that horse you were about to shoot."

Will took her hand and she pulled hard, helping him get to his feet. He stood, hugging himself, wincing in pain. "What business is it of yours?" he asked.

"Because I'm going to buy him from you."

He looked at her, past her at the horse, then back to her, and snorted derisively. "I was going to shoot it because it can't be rode. 'Specially not by a woman."

Emma. "Of course it can be ridden. Tell me. Where did you get him?"

"Some yonder man rode through a week ago. Said he was up in the Cimarron River country when he got jumped by a Kiowa. He kilt the Kiowa and took his horse. He come through lookin' for a job but Mr. Dundee wouldn't give him one. Sometimes drifters come south this time of year looking for a warm bunkhouse to winter in, then more often than not move on when green-up comes along. He wanted to sell the horse so I gave him ten dollars. My string is a couple of horses short. Thought I could break him. But he won't be broke, and he's no good to me as is, so I was going to shoot him."

Emma produced a twenty-dollar gold piece. "I'll give you this for him," she said. "Go on, take it." When the cowboy took the coin she walked over to the pen. Will and the other Double D hand followed.

"Lady, you're crazy if you think you can stay on that wild one," said the wrangler. "You ain't even wearin' spurs. You staying on that horse is a real longshot."

"You stayin' alive if you go in the pen is a longshot," opined the wrangler.

She was peering through the mesquite poles of the high fence at the pinto standing with his head only a few feet from the post, round which the rope on his neck had been wrapped numerous times. "He was an Indian pony. He wouldn't take to spurs. Though it looks to me like you gave him plenty. He's bleeding." She shed her duster, draping it over the top of the fence, and leaned her Winchester against the side of it. Will gaped at the twin Schofields as she took off the cross-draw holsters and draped them over her duster. As she began to climb over the fence the wrangler spoke up and began to climb, too.

"Hold on. Let me get a-holt of his ear before you try to get on his back."

"No," snapped Emma. "You stay away from him." She jumped off the top of the fence into the pen and the wrangler just shook his head and perched on the top rail. Will stopped looking at the gold coin and stuffed it into a pocket, climbing the fence far enough so he could drape his arms over the top.

"She's plumb loco is what she is, Will" declared the wrangler, then glanced at his *compañero*, a worried look on his face. "You reckon Mr. Dundee will get mad at us if she breaks her neck or gets trampled to death?"

Will didn't say anything.

Emma walked right up to the pinto, took the bridle off his head and dropped it on the ground. Then she gripped the lasso with her left hand and laid her hand on the horse's forehead, gently stroking down the face to the muzzle, talking softly. "They've given you a hard time, haven't they, boy. Well, that's all over and it won't happen again. You're mine now, and we're going to be fine. We're going to be good friends, you and me." The pinto jerked up its head, snorting Emma pulled down on the lasso, the noose snug around the horse's neck, and began stroking his face again. "Hush. It's okay now. You're going to be fine." She ran her hand over one of the horse's eyes and its head jerked up again, and again she pulled down on the rope. The next time she passed her hand over its eye it remained still. Letting go of the rope, she pulled apart his lips and checked his teeth. "You got all your teeth in, that's good. I can still see the cups but the corners are wearing a bit. I'd say you're around five years old. Is that about right, boy?"

Taking up the lasso in her left hand again, right up under the pinto's throat latch, she turned and gave it a tug and began walking slowly round the post. The horse didn't want to budge, but she kept tugging, and finally it came along. When it began to go ahead of her, she pulled back on the rope, and when it tried to shoulder her she pushed back steadily against its ribs behind the shoulder, laughing softly. "No, you can't be the leader," she told him. "You're going to have to follow my lead from now on."

She walked around the post a dozen times, heeding the horse, and in return getting it to heed her. When the pinto tried to jerk away she dug in her heels and leaned back and let the rope out a bit, then reeled him back in. Then they walked some more. Eventually Emma moved around to the port side, she checked the cinch of the old hull Will had been using and then put boot to stirrup and quickly climbed aboard. The horse lunged forward and started to lower his head, stiffening his forelegs. Emma settle into the saddle, pressing her heels down, turning the pinto's head sharply to the left by shortening up the left-side rein until she could see the side of his face, making him turn in a half-circle. At the same time she loosened up on the right-side rein. To tighten up on both would give the horse something to brace against and start bucking.

Opening up the left-side rein, she coaxed the pinto into a turn, but then he yanked his head down in order to put his weight on his forelegs and release a burst of power with his hind legs. Emma felt his back end coming up—a sense of airiness beneath her, but once he had his head down she didn't try to pull it up. She smiled, leaned back and relaxed, pressing with her legs to urge it forward, but the pinto would have none of that and she settled in for a wild ride. Bucking was a horse's defense mechanism, and she knew that to be thrown would just encourage more of it. She kept her arms loose and gave him his head until he started to lower it again, and then she tapped with her legs, trying to coax him into moving forward. At first the pinto resisted and stood in place, forelegs rigid, back legs kicking high. Emma felt its power beneath her and let it run through her. She never lost her seat, or the smile on her face. She didn't tense up and stayed in perfect balance on the horse's 'hurricane deck'.

"Well I'll be damned," said Will, staring in amazement.

The excited wrangler let out a whoop, admiring the movements of Emma's slender supple body. "Look at her go! I swear I'd let her ride me any time!"

The pinto bucked a moment longer, and every time his back legs came down she pressed with her knees and applied a modicum of pressure to discourage him from putting his head down again. She kept her body relaxed, knowing that if she tensed up and lost her seat the impact of the horse coming up would catapult her forward onto its neck—or into the air. Eventually the horse became discouraged and surrendered to her persistent request that he move forward. Snorting and tossing its head, it began to prance and then to trot, letting his rider channel his energy into horizontal rather than vertical motion, a half dozen circuits of the pen until she firmly checked reins and slowed him to a stop. Dismounting, she stroked its powerful neck, and started talking again.

"Well there you go," she said, admiringly. "That was a good try. But now you see that it won't do you any good. You belong to me now. And I belong to you." As she talked, in a soft, mellifluous tone, she began undoing the saddle cinch. The pinto turned his head to watch her. "I'll look out for you. You'll look out for me. That's how it works." She pulled the old saddle down on her side and let it drop to the ground. "We have a deal?"

She walked the horse thrice more around the pen and then to the gate near where the Double D hands had watched her ride. The wrangler clambered down off the fence to open it for her, but she beat him to it, and led the pinto through. She turned violet-blue eyes on him, a wry curl touching her soft lips.

"If I rode you I'd break you twice as fast," she said.

The wrangler blanched, mortified and speechless. He hadn't thought it possible that she would be able to hear his comment.

Looking on, Will remained on the fence, since the pinto was out of the pen. He guffawed at the expression on his compadre's face, then glanced at Emma. "I guess you was right and I was wrong. He's your horse alright."

Emma smiled happily as she tied the pinto a fence pole long enough to don her holsters and duster and secure the Winchester in its saddle boot. "Then we both came out ahead," she said, a reminder to Will that he had come out ten dollars to the good. "I think I'll name him...Longshot. Thanks, boys, for coming up with that." Armed and fully dressed again, she took up the reins and headed for the big house, the pinto coming along behind with just an occasional, unruly jerk of the head.

III.

Moments after going back inside the Double D ranch house, Cord was sitting at a long mahogany table and had a mug of hot fragrant coffee and a bowl of savory beef stew set before him. While he wolfed down the vittles, Dundee, who sat across from him, told his own story, how before the war he had come to Texas to get into the cattle business, betting on that being a better road to success than getting caught up in a war which he expected would ravage the East. He had expected Texas to remain out of the Confederacy, since slave labor had not been and never would be a big factor in the state.

Making a go of a spread like he wanted was a hard and perilous endeavor, what with hostile Indians, a lawless frontier, and the cattle fever that made it difficult to push herds through Kansas, where farmers and ranchers tried to enforce a quarantine against Texas cattle. He had lost one wife to disease and another in childbirth, trying to deliver a baby boy with the umbilical cord wrapped around its neck. He had one son, who was presently with most of the crew bringing cattle in off the far western range for the winter. Estella and her husband, Lopez, had been with him from the beginning.

"When I first staked out this place, Wolf Creek was just getting started, too," Dundee said. "Not much more than a trading post and forge in the beginning. I want to see it prosper as much as anyone. If it doesn't—if it dies—I have to haul my supplies from San Saba, and my men have to ride a day and a half instead of a few hours in the saddle to get somewhere they can blow off some steam. And that's something hired hands just have to do now and again."

"I know," said Cord. "I worked on a cattle ranch once, for a while."

"I didn't take you for a cowboy," admitted Dundee.

"I wasn't." Cord decided to reveal his true identity to the rancher. "I spent some months on the Tichnor Ranch in California, outside Sacramento. My sister and I were hired to take care of a rustling operation."

"You and your sister are regulators?" Dundee was surprised.

"I prefer to think of ourselves as problem solvers."

They were finished eating and Estella appeared right on cue, efficiently clearing the table before bringing some fresh coffee and cigars. Cord accepted the former but turned down the latter. As Dundee lit his cigar, puffing rings of smoke like a locomotive, he let his curiosity get the best of him.

"Then what brings you to these parts?"

"The army payroll."

"So now you're working for the United States government."

"We do, from time to time."

Dundee nodded, and his expression darkened. "I hope John Mackey pulls through. I like him. He's a fair man. Has nothing to prove. Some starpackers do, you know. Or the power goes to their head. They start provoking fights. They turn into bullies. Cowboys are prideful, and they won't stand for being pushed around too much. John understands that. And it's why Double D men are supposed to check their guns at the jail when they ride into town. I feel bad that one of my men shot him. But I guess I'm not surprised that it was Burt who done it. He had a chip on his shoulder. Folks wiped out by Comanches. He was an angry young man. No one gave him a chance because of that. I had reason to let him go more than once, but...I felt sorry for him, and kept him on the payroll."

Cord quietly listened to this rambling *mea culpa*. The fact that Dundee hadn't asked more questions about the army payroll and his and Emma's specific duties regarding it led him to believe he had been right to trust the man with the truth. When the rancher lapsed into morose silence, no doubt dwelling on the dead cowboy and the nearly dead lawman of Wolf Creek, Cord thanked the rancher for his hospitality and got up to go. Dundee walked him out.

The both stopped in their tracks when they saw Emma, covered with dust, securing the pinto to the back of the buckboard, which Johnny Lang had brought back around to the front of the ranch house after depositing Burt Riggins' body on the back porch.

"Isn't that the bronc that Will Taylor was trying to break?" asked Dundee.

"One and the same," replied Emma, leaning against the pinto, her arm draped up and over the horse's withers. "He's mine now. I bought him."

"Will broke that horse and then sold him to you?" asked Dundee, incredulously.

"No. He was going to shoot this horse, so I bought him."

"And you broke him?"

"I prefer not to think of it as breaking. Let's say this horse and I came to an agreement."

Smiling, Cord climbed up into the buckboard and threaded the reins through his fingers.

Dundee stepped up to the buckboard. "Should Mackey not make it, maybe you'll take to wearing the marshal's badge for a spell. Seems plain you can handle yourself in a tight spot."

Cord didn't have to wear it or touch it to be aware of the tin star he carried in a pocket. He hadn't told anyone that he had it, and glanced at Emma. She was watching him curiously. He looked back at the rancher and shook his head. "Thank you for your hospitality, Mr. Dundee."

The rancher extended his hand. Cord shook it again. Out here you shook a man's hand when you met and when you parted if you were still on good terms.

As Cord got the buckboard in motion, Emma glanced over her shoulder at the pinto and smiled, giddy with happiness.

CHAPTER FIVE

A Man Called Smith

I.

When Emma arrived at the general store the front doors were open but there was no one inside. She ventured down a short hallway in back, opening one door into what appeared to be a small storeroom, while a second door opened into a room with a small window that she took to be John Smith's bedroom, as it contained a narrow bed, a small table, a large chest, and nothing else. The door at the end of the hall opened to the alley out back.

She was wearing a black fitted jacket with a satin collar, sharp points in the front and a peplum at the back. The long sleeves were poufed at the shoulder and had deep satin cuffs. It was buttoned from waist to collar. The matching twill skirt showed off her slender form. On her feet were high-topped lace-up boots of black leather and gray brocade.

As she returned to the front of the store she heard a train whistle and glanced outside, smiling as she noticed that some people were making haste northward to the Texas & Pacific tracks on the outskirts of Wolf Creek. In time, the residents would think nothing of the arrival of a train but for now it was an exciting event.

The store itself was neat, organized and stocked to the rafters. A fairly new plate-glass window adorned the front of the business, with the words

SMITH'S MERCANTILE stenciled in flashy bold letters on it. A long table under the window was laden with crates of fresh produce and bolts of fabric. She surmised that both probably sold better when viewed in good light. Also in the front of the store was a potbelly stove with a few chairs ranged around it. Every western town had a place or two that wasn't a saloon where the locals preferred to sit and pass the time of day, especially in the cold weather months, and it looked as though in Wolf Creek the general store was one of those places.

Along the long south wall was sturdy shelving loaded with consumables: flour, rice, coffee. sugar, vinegar, eggs, raisins, honey, molasses butter, lard, salt, dried apples, peaches in airtights and more. On the floor were barrels of corn, various grains, beans, apples and carrots and cabbage and casks of salted beef and fish.

There were two counters along the north wall, the one closer to the door home to a cash register, coffee grinder and scales. On the walls behind it was an apothecary case containing patent medicines, elixirs, soaps, perfumes and colognes. A map cabinet stood beside this. The display case contained pistols, knives and timepieces. On the wall behind this were gun racks with rifles and shotguns, the shelves underneath loaded with ammunition.

On and under tables in the center of the store were dungarees, shirts, shoes and boots, long johns, blankets, linens, and baskets containing pins and needles, buttons, ribbons and thread. On the short back wall were tools, rope, lanterns, cooking utensils, and the doorway to a short hall leading to a storeroom and the room where Smith slept.

Emma was standing at the fabric table, looking out the window, tapping her foot impatiently, when a man strode through the door, took two steps, then saw her and stopped and looked. By then she had put a hand on a bolt of green taffeta. He was about thirty, she thought, a solidly-built, broad-shouldered man about five feet-ten inches tall, with light blue eyes and a thick, unruly mane of black hair streaks of gray at the temples. She decided she had gotten her wish—he was, all in all, a rather handsome man and so she smiled warmly.

"Hello," she said. "I hope you don't mind. The doors were open."

He smiled back and came closer. "Don't mind at all. When I have to go somewhere during the day I generally leave the doors open."

"You are a very trusting man."

"Well, I haven't been here in Wolf Creek for very long, ma'am, but long enough to know that the people here are good, honest people. A quiet place to live for the most part. Although that wasn't the case a couple of days ago."

"Oh yes, I heard someone say the marshal had been shot."

Smith grimaced. "Yep, by a local cowboy in one of the watering holes."

"How horrible. Did you see it happen?"

"No. By the time I got over there to have a look, the Marshal had been moved to Doc Haster's office. According to some of the people standing around outside, the doc was operating on him."

"I do hope he survives."

"As do I, ma'am."

"Miss. Miss Emma Remington." Since he was standing right in front of her by then she proffered a hand. Smith brought his hand up to rest hers in the palm and raised it to his lips. Her smile deepened.

"John Smith, Miss Remington. A pleasure to meet you."

"And a gentleman as well," she murmured, with a sparkle in her eye. "Please, call me Emma."

"Are you from these parts, Emma?"

"No, I just arrived the other day, with my brother."

Smith nodded. "I was going to say the gods must have been unhappy with me if you'd been in town all this time and I had not had the pleasure of making your acquaintance." He let go of her hand and moved past her to the potbelly stove. "Would you care for some coffee? I warn you, it has been on the stove since daybreak, so it's likely thick enough to float a horseshoe."

"I'm fresh out of horseshoes that need floating, but thank you."

Smith chuckled as he opened the stove's door and checked the fire inside, poking it into life with a stick taken from a box of wood that looked to Emma like broken pieces of a crate or barrel. Then he shut the door and poured himself a cup of the coffee. "Is there anything in particular you're looking for, Emma?"

"Oh, no," she made a little throwaway gesture. "I was simply whiling away the time. But if I were looking for something to purchase I think odds are excellent that you would have it in stock." She glanced admiringly around the store.

"Well for now anyway it's the only store of its kind in Wolf Creek, so I decided I needed to have everything I could get that the folks here might need."

"Then I would think you do pretty well for yourself, Mr. Smith."

He looked pensively around the store. "To be honest, I didn't think I would like being a storekeeper as much as I do."

"Oh? Why is that?"

"I was pretty much a yonder man after the war. Holding down one odd job after another. Hunter for a railroad, bringing in meat to feed the crews. Pushed a few herds of cattle in my time. Gun guard for a stage line. And before I ended up here I prospected for gold down in the Sierra Madre."

"You fought in the war?"

He nodded, looking out the window with bleak eyes. "That I did. Born and raised in Illinois, but then my folks moved out to Kansas. They were abolitionists. A lot of anti-slavery people moved to Kansas back before the war. Well, it's closer to the truth to say we had ourselves a war in Kansas long before First Manassas."

"Bleeding Kansas," she said.

"Yeah," said Smith, grimly.

Emma detected the raspy hollowness in his voice. It was the sound of someone who had suffered the kind of loss you never really could get over. She sensed she would get nothing more out of him about his wartime experiences, so she changed the subject.

"So then you became a drifter—a yonder man, as you say. Sounds ... romantic."

Smith smiled, and the way he looked at her convinced Emma that he took her for a rather naive young woman. "Hardly. A lot of cold lonely night camps. A lot of looking over your shoulder."

"But you must have done alright for yourself. I mean, you had the wherewith to buy this store, didn't you?"

"I didn't buy it. I won it in a poker game."

He put the empty cup down and walked over to the counter near the front doors, went around it to reach under it, pulling out a frayed and faded leather apron which he draped over his neck and then tied at the waist in back. By then Emma, who had followed, planted her elbows on the counter, her head in her hands, and was exclaiming. "Oh! That sounds like a good story, and I do love good stories. Do tell!"

"Well, I rode into town a couple of months ago with eight dollars to my name. I got a drink of whiskey at The Palace and then bought into a game of poker with what was left. To be honest, I didn't expect to be sitting at that table for very long. But an hour later I stood up with a couple of hundred dollars and the ownership of this store in my hands."

He told her that the previous owner, Abel Cushing, had been one of the early settlers of Wolf Creek. He had come with his wife and son and the desire to make a new life for himself on the edge of the frontier and by all accounts did quite well for himself. Then his wife died, and his son apparently wanted nothing to do with storekeeping and struck out to find his own way. Cushing turned to drink.

"I could tell he was drunk when I sat down," said Smith. "Too drunk to play poker. When he put the store up on account of he was short the cash to meet my bet, he wrote out a promissory note and added to the pot. Several of the people watching the game tried to talk him out of it."

But Cushing was a belligerent drunk, and when he started getting hostile with the men who were trying to look out for him, they backed off. Smith won the hand with three queens over two pair, kings high.

"When I won I tried to sell the note back to him for a fraction of what the store was worth. I guess my conscience was getting the better of me. Felt like I had taken advantage of the old man."

But, as Smith told it, his generous offer served only to enrage Cushing, who stood up so suddenly he knocked his chair over, then fell backwards over the chair as he struggled to get an old Colt Walker out from under his belt. A few of the spectators jumped on him and tried to wrestle the antique pistol out of his grasp but Cushing put up a fight and accidentally blew his knee to smithereens. He lasted until the next morning, refusing to let Doc Haster take his leg, which was his only chance for survival—albeit a slim one.

Smith told Emma he had expected a fair share of animosity aimed at him since Cushing was one of Wolf Creek's earliest settlers. But word spread about his willingness to essentially give the store back to the former owner, and then he found himself generally accepted. The store itself required a lot of work, as Cushing had lost interest in keeping it a profitable enterprise after his son had run off to California to find a berth on a whaling ship.. The time and effort—and the expense—of cleaning up and re-stocking the mercantile had not gone unnoticed, or unappreciated, by the populace. Smith had gone to Fort Worth and come back with three wagon-loads of merchandise bought with his poker winnings. It felt good, he said, to have a place he could call home after years of wandering. Felt good, too, not to have the weight of a pistol on his hip all the time.

Emma heard a wagon trundling along Front Street, and then then the gruff and profane shout of a man exhorting some mules to stop. "Whoa there, you goddamned knobheads! Whoa I said!"

"That's Loomis," said Smith, peering out the front window and catching a glimpse of the wagon slowing in front of the store. "Driver for Alamo Freight. He's got a pretty sour disposition. He says it's on account of his wife being overbearing. And that youngster with him is a hostler name of Stick. He is a wonder around horses. Even mules listen to him. I think that's why John Jacoby, the owner of Alamo Freight, overlooks the fact that Stick is half-Mexican and half-Tonkawa." He glanced at her to see if she had a reaction to that news.

Emma smiled at him, a somewhat querulous expression on her face. She knew it was, but decided it would be better to feign ignorance. "Is that an Indian tribe?"

"Yes, it is. The army employs them as scouts a good bit, since they have been enemies of the Comanches. But a lot of people—and most other Indian tribes—don't like them being around."

"Why is that?"

"Because they're cannibals. Not all the time, mind you, but they do eat human flesh now and again."

Emma made sure her eyes got big as saucers, and that a horrified expression inhabited her face. "Cannibals!"

"Don't worry, I'll make sure he doesn't eat you, Miss Remington."

"Emma. You're too kind." She waited until Smith was heading for the door, his back to her, before she rolled her eyes. Then she followed the store-keeper outside, narrowing those eyes against the brightness of the day. The sun was nearing its zenith. She watched a bearded portly reinsman wrestling with the reins to stop the pair of mules hitched to a heavily-laden wagon. He was still cursing up a storm—it wasn't always easy to get a mile started but once you did it was sometimes even harder to get them to stop.

"Hello there, Loomis, Stick," said Smith. "Have any trouble?"

The driver clambered down off the wagon seat and cast about for some shade, spotted just a ribbon of it provided by the slanted roof over the general store's porch and got into it, rubbing his eyes. "Hell no," he replied. "Every'body in these parts knows I carry a greener and I ain't shy about usin' it."

Smith chuckled. "No, I mean with the railroad, getting my merchandise."

"Oh that. No, sir. No problem at all." Then Loomis got a good look at Emma, and his eyes widened. "Damn me if you ain't the purdiest girl I think I ever did see. You ain't a soiled dove by any chance, are ya?"

Smith frowned at him. "Mind your manners, Loomis."

"Aw hell, I'm sorry, miss. It's my old lady's fault. She don't care to lay with me no more, and I don't wanna go without a poke now and then and I'm so desperate now I feel like goin' over the hill for good and just start payin' for it."

"Loomis!" snapped Smith, perturbed.

Emma debated whether to act offended, but suddenly she couldn't help but laugh. "It's quite alright, Mr. Smith, really." She smiled forgiveness at Loomis.

"*Como andas, Señor* Smith!" exclaimed Stick as he jumped down off the wagon. He was young and slight of build, with a big friendly grin that he turned on the storekeeper, then on Emma. "*El viejo tiene razon, Señorita! Eres la mujer mas hermosa de toda Texas!*"

Smith thought he should translate. "He said...."

"I know what he said, thank you. *Gracias*, Stick."

Stick flashed a guileless grin and turned to the wagon. "I think we got everything of the train that was yours, *Señor*."

"*Como siempre, muchacho*," replied Smith, and turned to Emma. "Pardon me, miss. I need to help move these goods inside."

"Oh, don't mind me, Mr. Smith," she said gaily and stepped to one side as the storekeeper turned to the wagon laden with crates and barrels and big burlap sacks. Stick unchained and lowered the tailgate and then both of them proceeded to carry the goods inside.

Meanwhile, Loomis did a slow 'walkabout' around the wagon. He belatedly became aware of Emma's wry smile. "I do this every time I climb down off a rig, whether the trip was a hunnerd miles or a hunnerd yards," he explained. By the time he got around to pitching in and helping Smith and the young hostler, the wagon was nearly empty, which gave Emma cause to wonder how much of the portly reinsman's meticulous examination of the wagon was dedication to his job and how much had been a pretense to avoid hard labor.

As Smith passed by her on the way to the door, a 50-pound sack of corn on his broad shoulder, he read her expression and glanced back at Loomis. "It's okay," he murmured. "Loomis is a might clumsy. But according to Stick there's no better driver in Texas, be it a Concord coach or a buckboard wagon, or anyone more savvy when it comes to handling a team of horses. Or mules.".

With the mercantile shipment unloaded, the wagon was still about a quarter-full. Loomis opened a worn leather dispatch case and consulted some of the documents therein. Emma assumed these to be documents pertaining to the shipments freighted to and from individuals and businesses in town, such as bills of lading and invoices. The reinsman was mumbling that he and Stick had a couple more stops, and detailed each one while he fumbled through the papers. Smith went inside the store and emerged a moment later, handing Loomis a block of chewing tobacco and handing Stick a bag. The hostler reached inside the bag and brought out a bunch of carrots and looked absolutely delighted. "*Muchas gracias, Señor* Smith!" he exclaimed.

Finding the Texas & Pacific bills of lading, Loomis gave one to Smith and then asked the storekeeper to sign another. Smith was prepared, producing the stub of a pencil and scribbling his name. A moment later Loomis and Stick were back on the wagon's bench and the former was profanely exhorting the mules to get moving. As the wagon trundled away, Emma glanced at Smith and asked, "Carrots? Does he eat them, or cut them up and add them to his cannibal stew?"

Smith chuckled. "He feeds them to the Alamo Freight horses. They're his family."

Emma looked after the wagon, liking the young half-breed sitting beside Loomis even more.

Smith walked inside, and she followed, her eyes locking onto two long crates at the bottom of a stack that consisted of small barrels and numerous wooden crates of various sizes. Smith went around the front counter and opened the cash register and put the bill of lading inside.

"How long are you and your brother going to be in Wolf Creek?" he asked.

"I'm not really sure," she said, thinking on her feet. "He is an agent for the railroad. Here to discuss rates and what not with the local merchants. I'm sure he'll be wanting to meet you."

"I will look forward to it. And you ... just came along to see the sights?"

Emma gave a little shrug of the shoulders. "I'm easily bored. I couldn't bear to stay behind."

"You do know that this is the frontier, don't you? There's nothing much west between here and the New Mexico Territory except rough country and bad hombres."

Thinking about the three hide hunters she had killed a few days earlier, Emma tried to appear as though she was hearing about the Llano Estacado for the first time. "Really! Well, don't worry, sir, I won't be venturing out of town."

Smith returned to the pile of goods and as he drew near her he pulled a sodbuster's folding knife out of a pocket of his apron, and with a flick of a wrist brought the five-inch blade out of the wooden handle. Acutely aware that this was one of the rare occasions when she wasn't carrying a firearm, Emma nonetheless stood her ground and managed to look untroubled, though her eyes became hooded and bright.

"Glad to hear it," said Smith, as he bent down to use the knife's thick blade to pry the lid off a crate. Glancing at its contents, he carried it to a counter. While his back was to her Emma bent down, too, and examined the side of one of the long crates. It was unmarked.

"Well," she said cheerfully, straightening, "I see you have a lot of work to do, Mr. Smith, so I will bother you no further. I enjoyed our little chat."

She was turning for the door when Smith spoke up. "If you're not doing anything tonight, Miss, I usually have dinner at the Continental Café. Maybe you would see fit to join me? Say around six o'clock?"

"I won't meet you, Mr. Smith," she told him, with a very serious look on her face. Then a smile began tugging at the corners of her mouth. "But you can *take* me to dinner. 'll be waiting in the lobby of the Longhorn Hotel to-morrow evening."

Smith smiled and nodded. "Where are my manners? See you then."

Emma checked for her brother at the Longhorn and then proceeded to the jail and walked in to find Cord conversing with a lanky, red-headed young man. Her brother held the town marshal's badge in the palm of his hand.

"I just wanted you to know that this wasn't my idea," Cord was telling the carrot-topped kid. Then he turned his head to see who was entering.

"Mercy, I hope not!" exclaimed Emma, aghast.

"Em, this is Toby Jukes, the marshal's deputy. Toby, this is my sister."

Toby was gawking at her, but Emma was accustomed to men staring. "How is Mackey?" she asked Cord.

Cord shook his head. "No news."

Emma broke the moment of grim silence by taking the star out of her brother's hand and pinning it to his shirt. "There. If you've got it, you might as well wear it. Doesn't mean it won't come off. Besides, might get you free drinks at The Palace."

"Reckon you wear it better than I could," said Jukes, looking and sound-ing relieved. "Being a town marshal ain't so bad, you know. There's more to it than handling rowdies or badmen who come to town. Not a day goes by that there isn't some quarrel between townfolk where one or all concerned didn't feel like the law should take their side. Last week a customer at the Cigar and Fine Liquor Emporium was dead certain Mr. Umbricht was cutting expensive whiskey with cheap rotgut. One of Ned Bohannon's customers hasn't paid his bill and Bohannon is threatening to sell the horse and the other man is threatening Bohannon. If it ain't one thing it's another."

"How...exciting," remarked Emma, dryly.

Jukes had been wringing the hat he held in his hands, and now put it on. "I'll go do a walk-around. Nice meetin' you, miss." He slipped past them and went out the door.

Cord looked at Emma and nodded towards the door. They stepped outside into briskly cold gusts of north wind and Cord was not surprised to see that Toby Jukes was making a beeline for The Palace, where Kitty worked.

"I'll let Willie out and see what he does," he said. "What about Smith?"

"To hear him tell it, just a drifter who seems to have taken to the life of a storekeeper like a duckling takes to water. But there's just one thing. He received a shipment of goods today which included two crates that look very much like the type guns are shipped in. I would be obliged if you got into the store tonight and find out what they contain. I didn't get a chance to. You won't have to worry about Smith. He's taking me to dinner at the Continental."

"Maybe he plans to sell them in his store."

Emma shook her head. "He already has a case full of long guns."

"I don't know who he would be running guns to with the Comanche problem solved. And even if he is, I don't see a connection with the business that has brought us here."

Emma smiled at him. "Just humor me."

"Of course. How's the new horse?"

"Oh, he's quite a handful."

"Just as you like them. A shame you're not as picky about men as you are when it comes to horses," he said, tongue in cheek.

Emma slapped his arm playfully and sashayed away. Cord looked glumly at the star on his shirt then went back inside the jail to free the town drunk.

CHAPTER SIX

Death of a Lawman

I.

It was thirty minutes after sundown when Cord arrived at Smith's general store, and the night shadows were gathering in alleys and doorways. He had been in his room earlier and heard the Longhorn's proprietor, Annie Pritchard, knocking on Emma's door and informing her that "a gentleman had come calling." He went to his window overlooking Front Street and waited until he saw Emma, arm in arm with John Smith, crossing the street, heading east for the Continental Cafe. He donned his longcoat and took a small leather case filled with a picklock's tools—picks, wrenches, rakes and the like—out of his saddlebags and stashed it in a pocket of the coat. His knives and the Schofield pistol in place, he ventured forth.

His sister had told him that the back door of the establishment had been barred during her visit, and he assumed it still would be. The small window she had spotted in Smith's room in back was too high up the wall for him to reach without benefit of a ladder, and too small for his broad shoulders anyway. That left the front door.

By now Front Street was no longer a bustling thoroughfare after sundown. The street itself was quiet but a slow careful survey of the boardwalks revealed a few people walking, and a couple of groups of people talking. The busiest spot was out front of The Palace, across Crockett Street from the hotel. The Continental Cafe, yellow light bright in its front window was located further east along Front, near the edge of town. The general store was about halfway between the two and he decided what he had to keep an eye out for were people taking an evening stroll. He had told Emma that he would need at least a half-hour, though with one look at the lock on the store's front door he knew he would be inside in a matter of minutes.

It was certainly not a Chubb Detector or Bramah Precision lock. Patented in 1818 by Jeremiah Chubb, England's foremost lockmaker, The Detector had soon become the most widely used lock in that country. It was so highly regarded, in fact, that in 1851, it had been used to secure the case in which the great 186-carat Koh-I-Noor diamond was kept in the Tower of London. As for the Bramah Precision, it was said that not one of those had been picked since its inception in 1790. The Bank of England itself depended on the Precision. The Precision's impeccable reputation was eventually sullied by a picklock extraordinaire named Alfred C. Hobbs, to prove that better locks were needed—like the ones made by his London lock-making firm of Hobbs Hart & Co.

As he selected a couple of tools from his case, Cord smiled as he recalled the day in San Francisco, six years ago, when he had successfully picked a Chubb Detector to win a wager he had engaged in with a bank president. This had come about thanks to a parlor trick he had perfected at the age of sixteen—namely having his left wrist and ankle, and the right wrist and ankle, shackled together, then picking the locks with just a single pick clenched in his teeth in under three minutes. The thing that made the Detector such a challenge was a built-in anti-lockpicking mechanism; if one of the pins was lifted higher than a key would lift it, a lockdown mechanism was activated.

Cord had the door unlocked in under a minute. He didn't look around, but just walked right in and closed the door behind him. Emma had described a pile of freshly delivered goods—crates, sacks, and the two long boxes that had made her suspicious—in the middle of the floor. There was no such pile now. He found a lantern, lighted it, and checked behind the counters. Then he went into the two back rooms, and found the boxes in the small storeroom. Returning to the front of the store, he appropriated a crowbar and used this to pry the lid off one of the boxes. Holding the lantern high, he gazed down at the rifles piled inside the box.

There had to be at least twenty guns in the crate. He spotted some old Slant Breech Sharps Carbines, a couple of Winchester 1866 "Yellow Boys", a

Springfield Allin "needle gun" and a couple of Henry Lever Action Rifles in the stack.

Prying open the second box, he found it filled with pistols and a few shotguns. He used the crowbar to hammer the boxes closed, put the crowbar back where he found it, blew out the lamp and returned it to its proper place, and went out, locking the door behind him. Standing there in the night shadows for a moment, he mulled things over.

Like Emma, he doubted that John Smith had bought all those guns to stock his store. But if he was gun-running, why would he be up here, now that the Comanche Wars were over? It would make more sense to try to sell them south of the border, or maybe further west, where other Plains tribes were still resisting the western expansion of the white man. He didn't see how being in the business of running guns could connect Smith with the gang that had a hankering for army payrolls. But there was one way to find out.

When Emma saw his brother walk into the Continental Cafe she sighed. Having already decided that she wanted to 'sleep' with John Smith—and that regardless of whether he was in league with the outfit that was after the payroll shipment or not—she had been clinging to the hope that Cord had found farm implements or some such thing in the boxes that had aroused her suspicions. Obviously, that was not the case. The only explanation for Cord pulling up a chair was that he intended to confront Smith.

Before Smith could question his purpose, Cord smiled and stuck out a hand. "Cord Remington. You must be John Smith, the storekeeper. My sister has told me a lot about you. But she didn't tell me why you have two crates of guns in your store."

Emma wasn't surprised by Cord's smiling but confrontational approach. It was a good way to catch a suspect off guard. So she kept her sea-green eyes fastened on Smith while she slipped a hand into her small beaded purse to touch the handle of the Remington Deringer she carried there. She wasn't one for praying, but she found herself doing just that now, not wanting to put a .41 caliber hole between Smith's eyes.

Smith had been in the process of using a fork to transport a slice of steak from plate to mouth when Cord proffered a hand and made his remark. He put the fork down slowly, looking from Cord to Emma and back again, and a sardonic smile curled the corners of his mouth. He sat back, gave Cord's hand a perfunctory shake and then rested both hands on the edge of the table.

"I take it you broke into my store," he said flatly.

"Yes. But I locked it up tight when I left."

Smith's eyes were cold as they turned on Emma. "Now I know why you were flirting with me. Why you let me take you to dinner."

She shrugged. "If it's any consolation, I would have wanted to go to dinner with you anyway."

"I take it you're not a business agent for the Texas & Pacific," he told Cord, drily. "Who *do* you work for?"

Cord brought out the letter signed by the President of the United States.

Smith read it and then looked at Emma. "I reckon you have one just like it."

Emma nodded.

"I had those guns transported up here because the people of Wolf Creek are going to need them, along with the ammunition of various calibers that came with them."

"Why?" asked Cord.

"Because I know the man responsible for the robbing of the army payroll a couple of months ago. His name is Arch Cullen, and if you know that name then you also know that the life of every man, woman and child in this town is in jeopardy." He slowly raised his hands to grab the lapels of his jacket and open it, so that the Remingtons could see that he wasn't carrying a shoulder rig. "And you should also know I'm not just a storekeeper."

There was silver badge pinned to the lining of his coat. It read: Pinkerton National Detective Agency.

II.

"Arch Cullen," murmured Cord. "They call him The Angel of Death."

"He earned that moniker. He was one of Bloody Bill Quantrill's lieutenants at Lawrence, Kansas." Smith looked round the cafe. More than half the tables were occupied, and the owner, Amos Chelico, and his waitress, Ivy, were hard at work taking and serving orders. He glanced at Cord and Emma. "Maybe we should talk about this in private." He stood up, threw some money on the table and walked out. The Remingtons followed. Smith was lighting up a Mexican cheroot, looking up and down the street to see if anyone was coming their way. No one was. He fastened his steely gaze on Cord.

"You look to be too young to have fought in the War. What do you know about the Raid on Lawrence, Kansas?"

Cord searched his encyclopedic knowledge of history. "Lawrence was founded by staunch abolitionists out of Massachusetts. They turned it into a hotbed of antislavery sentiment before the war. It was also the headquarters for Redlegs who conducted some pretty bloodthirsty raids against innocent Missourians in the name of undermining civilian support for the pro-slavery Bushwhackers."

Smith nodded. "There were other reasons for the raid. General Order No. 10, issued by United States General Thomas Ewing, which called for the detention of those believed to be giving aid to the Bushwhackers who were raiding into Kansas. A lot of people were arrested, including about a dozen women who were all under the age of twenty. Those women were hauled off to Kansas City and locked up in an abandoned house. The house collapsed because of a weak foundation. Four women were killed, including the younger sister of Bill Anderson, who would become one of Quantrill's most bloodthirsty lieutenants. A whole lot of lives had already been lost by that time, but something about those four innocent girls losing theirs hit the Border Ruffians hard. There was a lot of cold-blooded rage built up by the time they rode into Lawrence."

Cord nodded. He knew that the conflict in "Bloody Kansas" had been about much more than slavery. An element of revenge motivated both sides because civilians were made targets in that partisan war. And, too, many were the Bushwhackers and Jayhawkers who were happy to have the opportunity to steal and rape in the name of states' rights or abolition. Greed, lust and vengeance—with such motives it was little wonder that bloody carnage like that wrought in Lawrence on August 21, 1863 had become commonplace in the Border War.

"Quantrill brought four hundred and fifty men," said Smith, his voice bleak, his gaze far away. "And they were armed to the teeth. One saddlebag was recovered that carried about twenty loaded cylinders for a pistol. They converged on Lawrence in several columns and joined forces on the outskirts to launch the attack right before sunrise. One of their objectives was a large brick hotel on the highest point in town. That became Quantrill's headquarters, and from there he dispatched his followers in several groups. There were some specific targets. Men like James Lane, who had formed a battalion of Jayhawkers that, among other things, sacked the Missouri town of Osceola.

"Osceola and other atrocities provoked General Henry Halleck to accuse Lane of turning many formerly pro-Union people against the North. But the truth is, any person in Lawrence was a target. Before the day was out, nearly a hundred and fifty men and boys had been gunned down, many of them shot in the back. Nearly half the buildings were burned to the ground, including most of the businesses. Banks and stores were robbed and looted. Bill Anderson earned the nickname 'Bloody Bill' because of his actions that day. He was motivated by the need to avenge his sister's death in Kansas City.

"But as bad as Bloody Bill Anderson was, Arch Cullen was worse. He had already earned his nickname—The Angel of Death. There was certainly no shortage of cold-blooded killers among the Border Ruffians who attacked Lawrence that day. But none killed with such sadistic joy and efficiency as Cullen. It's on the record—they took testimony from some of the survivors—that it was Cullen who forced unarmed men to walk back into burning buildings to meet their deaths."

Emma's head was tilted as she studied Smith's expression, and listened carefully to his tone of voice. "As I recall, you told me you were born in Illinois but your folks were abolitionists who moved to Kansas. Did you lose someone in Lawrence that day?"

Smith's narrowed eyes glittered. "Yes," he said, his voice colder than the night air. "Several Ruffians were dragging my mother off to .... do things to her. My father tried to stop them. Eyewitnesses swear it was Cullen who shot his legs out from under him. He kept trying to get to my mother, so he crawled. They say Cullen laughed when my father pled for mercy for my mother, and then shot him in the back of the head. I was ...I was in Missouri that day. I had just signed on with the Third Kansas Volunteers."

"I'm sorry," murmured Emma.

"After the war Cullen went to Mexico, joined up with other Confederate leaders like Jo Shelby, John Magruder and Sterling Price. They wanted to start a new Confederacy down there. Emperor Maximilian gave them his blessing. A colony was established between Mexico City and Veracruz. They wanted to start others, and Cullen was a colonization agent up around Monterrey. Like I told you, Emma, I went to Mexico. I wasn't looking for gold in the Sierra Madres, though. I established myself as a gunrunner, sold guns to revolutionaries and Apaches. I was getting close to meeting Cullen himself when I heard he had come back north, was up among the Cherokees in the Indian Nations. The Cherokees had fought with the Confederates during the war so it's not surprising they welcomed him. I was on his trail when I heard about the payroll train hold up, with every soldier killed and the train burned. I knew it was Cullen's handiwork. I also knew he would be after the next one.

It would be a bigger haul, because now the soldiers in those forts out west are owed even more back pay. You see, he needs money to get the new colony started. A lot of money."

"I get all that," said Emma. "But I don't understand why he would attack the town and its residents."

"That's just what he and his men like to do," said Smith. "Lawrence wasn't the only town where citizens were murdered in cold blood and the town was burned to the ground. He will do it to Wolf Creek because he wants to. This town will be sacked. Not just the payroll will be stolen. Anything else of value will be taken. Men will be murdered, women raped, buildings put to the torch. You see, for a lot of these men, the war never ended. After the Lawrence raid, General Ewing dispatched a large force of Redlegs commanded by Doc Jennison to drive every resident out of four Missouri border counties and destroy their homes. That was a mission the Redlegs enjoyed carrying out, and that many Missourians have never forgotten—or forgiven. But it's not just that. Men who ride with Arch Cullen are just very bad men."

Emma's green eyes were dark and hooded, a furrow deepening at the bridge of her noise, as she thought that the war had never ended for John Smith, either. "What about you?" she asked, bluntly "Do you care about the people here? Or are you only out for revenge?"

"Finding Arch Cullen and being face to face with him one time—that's all I lived for since the war. I didn't care about anything or anyone else." He paused and looked up and down Front Street, marked by pools of golden lamp and lantern light. "But I've been here long enough to get to know the people."

Cord stood there, arms folded, brow furrowed, as he contemplated the likely whereabouts of Cullen and his men. "I'm curious about that badge you wear. How did you come by it?"

"A few years ago some Cuban revolutionaries showed up in Mexico trying to buy guns. Allan Pinkerton had been hired by the Cuban government to put down the revolution, and that led his men to me. I had a face to face meeting with Pinkerton himself, told him why I did what I did. We cut a deal. Ranchers and other businessmen north of the border didn't like that Apaches were being armed, and the government was trying to find and stop me and others who were smuggling guns south of the border. Pinkerton made sure I wasn't interfered with. In return I just kept doing what I was doing, only as his agent. That way Allen Pinkerton would get some of the credit if I managed to kill Arch Cullen—which, by the way, would deal a severe blow to the hopes for a New Confederacy."

Cord nodded. "That sounds like Pinkerton. Okay, so I was told that as soon as the shipment arrives a messenger will be dispatched to Fort Griffin. The commander there of will send a detail to pick up the pay his men and those of the other garrisons are due. Messengers will be sent from there to other posts further afield. If this is indeed what happens then the Fort Griffin detail would arrive in Wolf Creek less than a week after the payroll arrives. Assuming Cullen knows this, he isn't going to be hiding up in in the Indian Territory waiting for word that the payroll is here. He's going to be in hiding, reasonably close by."

"What are you thinking?" asked Smith.

"That the people need to know what's coming." He glanced through the cafe's big front window and looked at Chelico waiting on a table and laughing at something one of his patrons said. "We'll start with the town council."

Smith shook his head. "They won't take my word for it. People don't want to believe that Death is coming for them. We need more. We need to find Cullen and his camp."

"This is rough country," said Cord. "Would take days to effectively search it. I'm more confident than ever, now, that there is at least one spy in town. In fact, we thought it might be you. But whoever it is, we need to find him, and then we need to make him talk."

"Oh he'll talk," said Smith, grimly.

"And then?" asked Emma.

"Then we get ready for war," said Cord.

She smiled. That smile faded somewhat when John Smith touched the brim of his hat to her and announced he was going to get some sleep, then turned and headed in the direction of the general store.

"I'm sorry your evening didn't turn out the way you had planned," said Cord.

She shrugged, trying to appear utterly indifferent to this turn of events. But Cord saw right through her. "No matter," she said. "I need to clean my guns anyway. How long do you think we have?"

"They won't come until the train shows up. And since there won't be any telegrams sent, there's no way to know for certain when that will happen. It could be a few days, or a few minutes."

When they entered the lobby Annie Pritchard came out of her room before they could reach the stairs to the second floor. The expression on her face made Cord stop in his tracks.

"What's wrong, Annie?"

"You didn't hear? John Mackey died tonight."

III.

John Mackey was buried at noon the next day.

Doc Haster had done everything in his power to keep the town marshal alive. That he had failed didn't surprise Cord. A gut-shot man rarely ever got back on his feet.

He was present when Mackey was laid to rest in the cemetery on the outskirts of town, standing with just about every townsperson and others from further afield, gathered to show their respect for a good man generally liked by all. They stood in the shade of young oaks raining dead, curled up leaves after every gust of a blustery north wind shook the treetops while Wolf Creek's preacher, a young Irishman by the name of O'Clary, read some scripture, spoke briefly to extol the virtues of the deceased, and then led the congregation in reciting the Lord's Prayer.

One person who wasn't present was Emma. Cord's sister disliked funerals. She had accompanied him to New Orleans, where together they had paid their last respects at the final resting place of their father. But from that day on Emma had avoided funerals and cemeteries. Cord surmised that the powerful emotions she had experienced at Silas Remington's gravesite had troubled or frightened her to such an extent that she refused to risk exposing herself to them again. Some thought her cold-blooded when it came to death. Cord thought it was more complicated than that. Today she was at Bohannon's Livery, using one of the pens there to work with her new pinto horse.

When the ceremony was over Cord stood there awhile. The marshal's star remained in the pocket of his coat, but he thought that the word of who carried Mackey's badge had spread, based on the way some of those present looked at him. As a whole they were curious but wary, and he didn't blame them. He was a stranger, after all.

After all the mourners had moved on, leaving only the preacher and the gravediggers, who awaited a sign from the former that they could lower the coffin into the hole they had started digging at dawn. Cord approached the pine box and put the first edition of Thomas Hardy's *Far from the Madding Crowd* on top of it. This was the book Mackey had been reading when they had met.

"You wanted to know who finally won Bathsheba's hand," he murmured.

"Well, after Sergeant Troy was murdered by Brownwood, who was committed to an asylum, Bathsheba turned to Gabriel Oak, the one suitor who had demonstrated he was willing to forego his own happiness to insure hers. They were wed. A happy ending."

Cord walked out of the bone orchard depressed, which was an uncommon mood for him. Mackey had seemed like a good man, and he'd had a good and inquisitive mind, else he would not have been reading Thomas Hardy. In the West, it was rare to find anyone who read more than the local newspaper and the dime novels that had been proliferating since the publication of *Maleaska, The Indian Wife of the White Hunter*, the first of the Beadle Dime Novels published in 1860. In England only the upper class had the leisure to develop an interest in literature. In America, the land of a free working class, there was no time for more than quick and easy entertainment.

Idly strolling in the general direction of the jail, Cord stopped abruptly and turned around to go back to the end of Front Street, then turned right, skirting some buildings until he reached a dirt track that brought him to a high embankment overlooking Wolf Creek. He turned left and passed through a small stand of scrub oak and cottonwoods, heading down a rock-strewn slope to the bend in the creek, where it turned westward., A row of eight shanties stood along the south bank of the creek. They were out of sight of the decent women in town, but probably not out the minds of their men, he mused.

The creek gamboled noisily through its rocky course. To the north of it was a steep slope thick with brush and young trees—an area he presumed was the source for much of the timber the town had and still did require. At the bend some large stones had been thrown into the water to provide a primitive foot bridge, the means by which a person could cross to reach the shanties without getting his boots wet.

Dulcey Garnet had told him she lived in the last shanty, and Cord headed that way. The gruff laughter of a man reached his ears from inside one of the buildings, and the gasping cries of a woman at the height of passion—or pretending that she was—from another. A slender and pretty mulatto was leaning against the door frame of another, smoking a corncob pipe. The frayed blue robe she wore was open enough for Cord to see a long caramel-brown thigh. The smile she turned on him faded as he moved on by with just a touch of his hat brim.

When he reached the last shanty, the door creaked open on rusted hinges and a smile was forming on his face—a smile that froze, half-finished, as a cowboy emerged, still hitching up his trousers and buttoning them. He glanced at Cord with a silly grin on his somewhat flushed face, and Cord caught a whiff of whiskey mingled with a perfume that smelled like lavender. The cowboy tossed a thumb over his shoulder and mumbled, "That yeller-haired one's a frisky filly, mister," and winked before moving along. He looked like he was late getting somewhere and apparently had walked over from town. Had a cayuse been hitched to the post in front of the shanty, Cord would have had some warning that Dulcey Garnet was 'entertaining'.

Watching the cowboy walking away with a quick, horse-warped gait, Cord experienced something that had rarely afflicted him—jealousy. He knew this couldn't be a product of love. How could a man fall in love with a woman he had met only once before, and that for no more than five minutes? Besides, only a fool would fall in love with a soiled dove, and he believed himself to be nobody's fool. He knew what the poets and the writers said about love—that it was something beyond a person's control, that it was unpredictable and could strike at any moment and without rhyme or reason. A person, they said, didn't have much say when it came to who he fell in love with. Cord grimaced and shook his head, bewildered. No, he couldn't be in love. Infatuated, maybe. Even so, he harbored second thoughts about coming here, and was considering leaving when the shanty door creaked open again.

Dulcey stepped out, wrapped up in a quilt, her smoky hazel eyes filled with delight at seeing him, her warm smile banishing any doubt on his part whether he should stay.

"Mr. Remington," she said, sounding quite delighted. "I was wondering when you would come."

He smiled wryly. "When...not if?"

She laughed softly, stepping closer, then unwrapped the quilt from around her body and handed it to him with a mischievous twinkle in her eyes.

"Would you mind terribly holding this for me?" she asked.

He took the quilt and she moved on by, walking naked and unabashed to the creek, where she sat on her heels in the shallows, tights spread wide apart to wash herself. Cord decided that she didn't squat like that to be brazen. She just didn't think anything about it. He supposed a woman who had been seen naked by who knew how many men would not be the modest sort or give much thought to propriety. He couldn't help but stare, admiring the curve of her spine, the flare of her hips, the heart-shaped posterior pale as alabaster in the bright daylight. She glanced over her shoulder and caught him staring, but he wasn't the least bit embarrassed.

With a salacious little smile tugging the corner of her mouth, she asked, "Why are you staring at me so? I'm sure you have seen a naked woman before. Probably many."

"Thinking about a verse from Sir Edmund Spenser's *The Faerie Queene.* 'She bathed with roses red and violets blue/And all the sweetest flowers that in the forest grew.'"

"How romantic!" Her smile was bright and warm like sunshine. "You're an educated man, aren't you, Mr. Remington." She glanced up the tall slope across the creek, scanning the tree line.

He looked that way, too, then at her. "Something the matter?"

She shrugged bare shoulders. "The last week or so I've seen a man up there. Well, not one man, at least two different men. Just standing up there watching."

He glanced over his shoulder at the mulatto girl still in the doorway of her shanty, and then at Dulcey, boldly, from head to toe. "Well, I can't say I blame him. Probably just a hunter who lives up there in the woods. Are you worried?"

"No. I have a Sharps pepperbox derringer. Not on me, of course."

Cord laughed. Considering the mood he had been in a little while ago, he was surprised that he *could* laugh. "I was at John Mackey's funeral. Left there feeling....out of sorts." Being someone who rarely wore his feelings on his sleeve, he felt uncomfortable opening up to Dulcey. But there was something about her that made a man want to unburden his soul.

Intently studying his face while he spoke, Dulcey nodded. "Those things gets us thinking about our own mortality," she murmured softly. "I liked the marshal. He was always fair-minded when it came to us who live down here along the creek. I would have attended but, well, all of Wolf Creek's godly folk would have been offended. And you know how godly some people become when they're at a burying. The last thing they want to see is a whore, a Jezebel, the Devil's Harl-..."

Cord abruptly wrapped an arm round her slender waist and pulled her to him, planting a hard, passionate kiss on her full red lips, and she was draping her arms languorously around his neck, rising up on the balls of her muddy little bare feet and leaning her slender, naked body eagerly into him as that kiss lingered.

When at last their lips parted she whispered breathlessly, "Let's go inside and help each other remember how good it is to be alive."

He swept her off her feet and carried her into the shanty. The creaking door had swung nearly closed and he kicked it open. Once inside, a single stride brought him to the narrow bed with its tousled sheets and he laid her on it. She bounced right back up onto her feet and took him by the wrists and turned him around and then pushed him down to sit on a battered old steamer trunk.

"What are you doing?" he asked, baffled.

She rubbed the day-old stubble on his cheek. "You forgot to shave this morning."

He rubbed his chin ruefully. "You're right. I found out about Mackey last night. Just had a lot on my mind this morning."

She looked at him, head tilted quizzically. "What else, besides the marshal's passing?"

Of course she couldn't know about Arch Cullen. For now, only he and Emma and John Smith knew—and probably one other person, the spy he was still convinced was lurking in or around the town. Then he realized that even when the news got out and spread like wildfire through Wolf Creek, it might not find its way to the creek-side shanties since the whores who occupied them were outcasts, and in times of danger most townfolk would not give them a second thought..

"Might be some men in these parts who plan to steal an army payroll shipment that's due in on the train in the next day or two."

"Why is an army payroll shipment coming here? How many men?"

"The United States Army sends the pay for the soldiers garrisoned in frontier forts west of here by rail to Wolf Creek, since, for now, this is the railhead. As for how many men, might be as many as fifty. Not sure. But more than enough to get the job done."

She looked at him, brows furrowed, silent for a moment. Cord could tell she had many questions, and he could surmise what some of them were. How did he know about the army shipment? Was that the reason he had come to Wolf Creek? Did he intend to stand and fight? Was he going to have to stand up to the robbers on his own? Was he willing to die to protect the army's payrolls? To her credit, though, she gave voice to none of these questions. Instead she turned and began to stir up some lather in an ivory shaving bowl bearing the shape of a pale blue bird.

"I have tender skin, you know," she said, with a soft, sidelong smile at him. She carried the bowl with brush inside it, along with a towel, over to him, draping the towel over his shoulder before lathering his left cheek and below the jawline. Putting the bowl and brush down, she picked up a straight razor laying on the small side table next to the bed. She ran the fingers of her free hand through his thick mane of unruly hair and then pulled his right cheek against her bare belly, holding it there while she proceeded to shave the left side of his face. Cord wrapped an arm loosely round her legs and closed his eyes. He inhaled deeply, dragging the smell of her skin, the scent of lavender from her perfume and—even though she had washed herself in the creek's shallows—just the hint of the musky aroma of sex.

Dulcey began scraping the whiskers off his face, regularly wiping the razor's blade clean on the towel. Even with the threat of Arch Cullen looming, Cord experienced a moment of calm and contentment with his cheek against her warm smooth belly, the scent of her filling his lungs, and those fingers gently massaging scalp. Dulcey Garnet, he thought, was no ordinary frontier whore. She was more a courtesan, accomplished in a number of ways, all useful in seeing to not just the sexual needs of men but their emotional well-being, too. Many of the soiled doves he had met had empty eyes, women who had little or no joy of life left in them, and who did what they did just to survive. He knew a few, though, who managed to hold onto a zest for life. Many of these aspired to better things. As for Dulcey, he struck her as someone who was smart, full of life, and better educated than most frontier whores. Apparently, she read the *Wolf Creek Chronicler*—the recent edition lay on the worn planking of the shanty's floor, between the bed and the small wood stove that kept the wintry chill at bay, opened in such a way that made clear she had been reading it—that it wasn't just paper to burn to start a fire. He wondered if she aspired to being anything other than what she was. She struck him as someone who genuinely enjoyed the company of men, of pleasing them sexually and otherwise. Apart from that, he didn't know anything about her, and decided to change that.

"You told me when we met on the street that you're from Virginia," he said. "How did you end up in this line of work?"

"How? Well, that's simple enough. I didn't listen to my mother. When I was sixteen I met this man, a lawyer, and thought I had fallen in love. He was moving to Kansas City. Said there was a lot more opportunity for a lawyer there. My mother told me not to go. She warned me that he would get bored with me and then leave me to fend for myself. Of course I didn't believe her. I thought she was making things up to keep me home." Dulcey smiled pensively. "I thought we were going to be married. But he kept putting it off.

Then he did *get* married. Just not to me. I found myself out on the street. I wrote home. My mother wanted me back but my father didn't." She paused, then added, her tone melancholy, "I suppose you've heard this story, or something like it, before."

While she recounted the story of her life, he had glanced at the bedside table and saw the half-full bottle of laudanum there. She noticed this, and added, "Sometimes I get a bit of the black dog, and that helps."

Cord nodded. Laudanum—ten percent opium and ninety percent alcohol—had been first used by the Greeks. Then as now it was a potent painkiller, sleep aid, and tranquilizer. Women were routinely prescribed laudanum for menstrual cramps, and nurses even gave it to babies who didn't feel good. "You're in good company. It's said that Samuel Taylor Coleridge wrote *Kublai Khan* when he awoke from a laudanum-induced dream. In fact, many artists—writers, poets, composers—relied on it."

Finished with his left cheek, she tightened her grip on his hair and lifted his head a bit to get to his neck. Now he could look up between her pert young breasts at her lovely face. She smiled down at him, and this time there was a wanton smile on her soft lips, and her eyes were smoky with desire. "Oh, well, I'm an artist, too. As you are about to find out, Sir."

He took hold of her hand, the one with the razor, taking the instrument from her and putting it on the bedside table beside the shaving bowl. He wiped his face with the towel she had draped over his shoulder and the tossed it away. Then he spun her around like they were waltzing, then let her go, and she fell back onto the bed, arms and legs akimbo.

Propping up on her elbows, on leg straight, the other with knee bent and allowed to fall to one side, Dulcey offered herself fully. With her alabaster skin, her perfect form, her golden curls, bright eyes and luscious lips she was, Cord decided, the kind of beauty the likes of which the gods of ancient Rome or Greece would have come down to possess. The dependency on laudanum had yet to take its toll on her looks. Thankfully, this vision made it impossible for him to mull over her words. With great urgency he yanked off his boots and shucked his clothes ... and then he was on her, and she squealed with breathless delight.

IV.

When they were done, Cord lay there awhile tangled up in twisted sheets and her warm smooth limbs, her head on his shoulder, her fingers gamboling through his chest hair, and he was as content as he had been in a very long time. But he couldn't keep thoughts of Arch Cullen and the army payroll quashed for long. She seemed able to read his expression and asked him what was wrong.

"I was just wondering how many other men you shave."

Her eyes became hooded, her expression inscrutable. "You shouldn't ask that kind of question," she said flatly.

"I'm not asking out of jealousy," he said, although he did feel a pang. He reckoned she was being mindful of his feelings, but in trying to protect his feelings she had made it clear he wasn't the only one. After that, exactly how many others didn't really matter. She was, no doubt, the most popular whore in Wolf Creek. How could she be otherwise? "I'm just wondering if you shouldn't get out of town. It's not safe here right now."

"Well, unless the soldiers decide to hide this payroll shipment under my bed I don't think I'm likely to be in the line of fire," she said wryly.

"I'm serious, Dulcey. The men who are after that payroll are very bad characters. No one is safe, especially not a woman as pretty as you."

She accepted the compliment with a soft smile. "Who are these men?"

"Well, the leader, and probably some of the rank and file, were Border Ruffians during the war. They raped, robbed, murdered and burned entire towns down to the ground. They'll probably try to do the same here."

She was alarmed, but even before she replied he knew what she was alarmed about. "Then you have to get out of here too!"

"I have a job to do." He disentangled himself and moved to the pile of his clothes and pulled a roll of greenbacks from a pocket of his long coat, detached a few and offered them to Dulcey. "Here's a hundred dollars. Enough to take you anywhere in the country you want to go. Take it, and leave Wolf Creek, please."

She looked at the greenbacks—more money than she had ever seen at one time—but she didn't take them. "Then I would never see you again."

"When you're settled somewhere write me. Cord Remington, La Fonda Hotel, Santa Fe, New Mexico Territory."

"And what if I showed up in Santa Fe?" she asked, with a pensive little curl on her lips.

"Then you *would* see me again. But there would be long periods when I would have to be away."

She nodded. "I wouldn't expect to have any hold on you, you know."

"Nor I on you," he said as he began to dress. Objectively, he thought Santa Fe would be a good place for a woman like Dulcey Garnet. He could see her becoming a highly sought- after courtesan, perhaps the mistress of some well-to-do man. But he wasn't sure he could be so nobly altruistic if they lived in the same town.

She remained quiet while he dressed, sitting up in bed, not bothering to cover herself, and looking pensive as she watched him. He bent over and kissed her, passionately, and pressed the greenbacks into her hand.

"Take the money," he said. "Go to Santa Fe if you like. It might take you a fortnight. You'll go east to Shreveport, then north to Wichita, then west to La Junta and finally south to Santa Fe by way of Lamy. You'll be switching from line to line, and might have to wait a couple of days for a train here and there. But there's plenty money to travel first class if it's available, with some left over."

"And there are no conditions?"

"I just want you to stay alive, Dulcey." He touched her cheek. "I better get going."

She nodded, quietly dismayed, but when he turned to the shanty door and opened it, she came off the bed and grabbed him from behind, her arms locking round his midsection. She lay her head between his shoulder blades and said, "Don't you die on me, Mr. Remington. I will never forgive you if you do."

CHAPTER SEVEN

The Angel of Death

I.

Reaching Front Street, Cord paused in the shade of the boardwalk and surveyed the thoroughfare from one end to the other. There was more than a score of people visible on the street. A pair of horsemen rounded a corner off a side street onto Front and he watched them a moment until he could see that they were cow hands. Then he started breathing again.

He believed John Smith's story. It explained a lot of things, for instance, the number of men who had attacked the train carrying the prior payroll shipment, and the fact that they had slaughtered every soldier in the detail and then put the train to the torch. The slaughter and the burning seemed like an act of war, or vengeance. No ordinary highwaymen would go to such lengths.

To keep forty or fifty men together required a charismatic leader. In the 1850s Joaquin Murrieta had terrorized California with a large group of friends and relatives who engaged in horse stealing on a large scale. They also attacked Anglo settlers and wagon trains. They killed over forty Chinese laborers and a dozen Anglos before they were tracked down by the California Rangers—an organization formed for that express purpose. Murrieta believed he was fighting a war. Cord wondered if Arch Cullen was still fighting his own war against the federal government.

Wolf Creek was bustling with activity now. People were on the move, afoot and on horseback. A wagon trundled by. It was essentially the same scene that had confronted Cord the day before, and the day before that. But it wasn't the same. He had the uneasy feeling a person would get if he saw a rattlesnake slither out of sight into tall grass, knowing death was near at hand, and it made things worse, not better, because he couldn't see it. Arch Cullen was that rattler.

Turning right, he passed in front of the barber shop and was about to walk by the Palace Saloon on his way to the jail when he suddenly changed his mind and went inside.

A man named Burl, a former pugilist, was tending bar. Cord had met him when he and Emma had stopped in their first night in Wolf Creek and they had shared some tales from their prize-fighting days. Burl had been a successful fighter until someone had busted the fingers in his right hand, which were now crooked and pretty useless because of all the scar tissue that had built up around the joints. He had cauliflower ears and a thrice-broken nose, trophies of his days as a bare-knuckle fighter. He grinned at Cord like he did everyone else who came up to the long mahogany bar, revealing that most of his teeth had been knocked out. Despite his bad hand, he could still handle drunken cowboys with his left hand and brute strength, though sometimes he resorted to a bag filled with sand weighted with a few smooth river stones.

Cord bought a bottle of Old Crow and carried it and a shot glass to a table near one of the plate glass windows adorned with the name of the establishment. To make sitting in the chair more comfortable, he pulled the Schofield out of his belt and laid it on the table. Three cowboys from the Cyclone, which as a cattle spread was second only to the Double D in terms of stock, if not size, were at a nearby table playing five-card draw, with one of the bar girls hovering around them. Kitty was at the far end of the bar flirting with a large bearded man with the look of someone who had spent his entire adult life out in the elements.

For half an hour Cord say at the table, drinking slowly and watching the street, until Burl bellowed out the hour. Two o'clock. The boxer-turned-bartender had a Sunderland pocket watch which he consulted regularly, and for some reason known only to himself called out every hour on the hour while he was on duty, without fail. It had become such a trademark of the Palace that other barkeeps had been instructed to do likewise.

Cord realized that he was burning daylight, that he should have been out trying to discover the location of Cullen and his men. But the enormity of the problem that confronted him, and the possibility—if not likelihood—that he would die when he came face to face with it, worried him a little, because he knew there was no way Emma would let him conduct the search alone. Her life was more important to him than his own.

He wracked his brain trying to come up with some way to accomplish four goals—keeping innocent people from being slaughtered, putting Arch Cullen down for good, saving the army payroll, and keeping himself and his sister alive.

His blue eyes swept the people in the room. The Palace was busy just about all the time after high noon, and now there were more than a dozen male patrons and four saloon girls in the place. There were good men in Wolf Creek. Men who would stand and fight for their livelihoods and the lives of their friends and loved ones. Some no doubt had fought in the war. But that had been true in Lawrence, Kansas back in 1863, too. Admittedly, the massacre at Lawrence had been carried out by four hundred Bushwhackers, but Quantrill hadn't needed that number, or even a quarter of that number, to succeed in sacking the town. There was no escaping the truth. If the people of Wolf Creek tried to stand against Cullen and his followers, some of them were going to die.

But it wasn't hopeless. There were several unknown factors involved. Just how many men were riding with Cullen. Could it be as many as fifty, as that Seminole scout had reported following the first robbery? And how large was the army detail protecting the payroll that was due to roll into Wolf Creek? And then of course there was Emma and himself. No, this wasn't going to be like Lawrence, Kansas on August 21, 1863. This wasn't going to be a slaughter. It was going to be a fight. One hell of a fight.

Corking the bottle he had bought, Cord looked over at Kitty again, and saw that she was taking the bearded man by the hand and leading him upstairs. Another man willing to pay a dollar for a poke. He thought about Toby Jukes, who had to know what men did with his girl while she was on the job. Toby was in love, or so he said. Having experienced a very uncharacteristic bout of jealousy himself earlier that day during his time with Dulcey, Cord wondered how Toby dealt with the feeling. Or maybe the boy was just grateful for Kitty's attention and was willing to accept any and all conditions to the relationship. This led to Cord speculating on the nature of his relationship with Dulcey if indeed she did show up in Santa Fe. Then he shook his head and silently scolded himself. He enjoyed Dulcey Garnet's company and just wanted to get her out of harm's way, and that was all. He wasn't in love. He didn't have time for love. Love was a distraction he could not afford in his line of work. And he especially could not afford to be distracted right now, so he tried to put the beautiful blonde whore out of his mind.

Leaving the Palace, Cord once again scanned the streets, standing at the intersection of Front and Crockett, the center of Wolf Creek. It was then that he noticed the bank, standing on the corner diagonally across the intersection from the saloon. For the first time he noticed something that made the bank different from the other structures he could see. It was made of stone—limestone by the looks of it—whereas every other building he could see from where he stood was made of lumber. It had two stories, with two windows and a door downstairs and two windows upstairs. The east side was solid stone from front to back.

He crossed the busy intersection to get a closer look, laid his hand on one of the masonry blocks used in long and short quoining on the corner of the building, Quoins gave the impression of strength to a structure that already looked quite sturdy, in stark contrast to some of the clapboard false front buildings usually seen in frontier towns. One thought kept rolling around in Cord's mind.

Cullen could burn the whole town of Wolf Creek down to the ground—except for this building. This building could stand up to him.

A man in a brown frock coat, tall and narrow-shouldered with a pot belly, emerged from the bank and walked closer, smiling broadly, thumbs hooked into the pockets of his vest.

"Good afternoon, sir! I couldn't help but notice that you were admiring the construction of this establishment. The First Bank of Wolf Creek has been built to last, as you can see. We intend to be here for decades, helping this frontier town grow and prosper." He extended a hand. "My name is Benjamin Dole. I am the manager. To whom do I have the honor of speaking?"

Cord transferred the half-full bottle of Old Crow from his right hand to his left and shook Dole's hand, introducing himself. Dole's eyes widened. "Ah, so you are the man who shot down the killer of John Mackey. Well done, sir, well done. And now I believe you are Mr. Mackey's handpicked successor."

"Temporary replacement."

"Yes, of course. As you may know, in most counties the sheriff is elected by popular vote, while the town marshal is selected by the mayor or, more often, the town council. Such is the case here in Wolf Creek. Soon I suspect the council will meet to debate and decide on Mr. Mackey's replacement. I think my fellow councilmen all agree that the town's chief peace officer should be an upstanding citizen, beyond reproach. A paragon of virtue. A symbol of all that is proper and righteous in the world."

"Well yes, ideally," said Cord, thinking about at least a dozen starpackers he knew personally or had heard about who had earned considerable notoriety, just since the end of the war. "As for a paragon of virtue, I sure don't fill those boots. So the sooner you and the council find the right man for the job, the better I'll like it."

He heard a train whistle.

It had been the sound he had been waiting to hear for days, and now it made his heart lurch in his chest. He looked north, up Crockett Street, in the direction of the tracks, and saw a plume of black smoke above the intervening buildings that no doubt billowed from a locomotive's smokestack.

"I've got to go, Mr. Dole," he said, and broke into a run. "But I'll be back!" he called over his shoulder.

He ran all the way, pausing only long enough to drop the bottle of whiskey in the lap of an oldtimer sitting on a bench in front of a barber shop. He didn't see the oldtimer pick up the bottle, read the label, then pull the cork and raise the bottle in his direction, a silent toast, before taking a long pull.

By the time he reached the station the train had come to a stop on the secondary line that ran parallel to the main line about two hundred yards. At either end of the secondary line were wheelhouses designed to turn locomotives and other rolling stock around. The secondary line was joined to the main line beyond the wheelhouses.

The train consisted of the mogul, a coal car, two flatbed cars carrying soldiers and sandbags stacked waist high on both sides, a freight car sandwiched between these two, a passenger car and a slat-sided livestock car forward of the caboose bringing up the rear. Cord did a quick head count. Twenty-one soldiers were in the fortified flatbed cars. A man with captain's bars on his tunic was hammering his fist against the door of the freight car, which opened to reveal several more enlisted men. Then the captain mounted the station platform and was met by a railroad man in a suit who emerged from the station itself to meet him. Cord approached them both.

"Captain Franklin Bolt, 18th Infantry Regiment," said the officer. "I am here on army business, Sir."

"Yes, yes," said the Texas & Pacific man. "Welcome to Wolf Creek, Captain. I received word of your imminent arrival by messenger from Fort Worth yesterday."

At least, thought Cord, they hadn't used the telegraph line that ran alongside the iron road all the way from Fort Worth to Wolf Creek.

"The train will remain here for at least a couple of weeks, Sir," said Bolt. "My men will bivouac on the far side of the tracks. I am authorized to inform you, under strict confidence, that we are escorting a large payroll shipment for forts along the Texas frontier. A dispatch rider will set out today for Fort Griffin. The commander there will send a large force to transport the payroll by wagon from here to there. Then the train will depart."

Hearing this, Cord realized someone in the U.S. Army chain of command had made a smart move, deviating from the standard procedure of notifying several garrisons to send a detail to pick up their share of the payroll and limiting it to just one, the nearest garrison.

"Of course, Captain. I will inform the mayor of your arrival. If you or your men need anything at all, please just let me know and I will pass...."

Bolt had noticed Cord's presence and was staring at him suspiciously, and the station man stop talking and did likewise. Cord already had the letter Colonel Bronson had provided him in hand, and he presented it to the captain.

"Don't mind me, gentlemen," he said, with what he hoped was a disarming smile. "Cord Remington, and you could say I am here on official business, too."

He monitored Bolt's expression as the captain read the letter bearing the presidential seal and signature and before Bolt was done reading he could tell that the officer was going to resent the hell out of him if he started throwing his official weight around.

"So," said Bolt, returning the letter. "You are basically the president's agent." He didn't sound very impressed.

Cord glanced past Bolt as the livestock car was opened up and a half-dozen horses were led down a ramp. He assumed these were for the dispatch riders destined for Fort Griffin, and that Bolt was sending more than one—and each probably towing a remount—by different routes to ensure that the message arrived at its intended destination.

Moving to the window where the telegrapher, a chubby young man, was seated, he said, "Check to make sure you still have a wire to Fort Worth." As the telegrapher tapped a quick message on his key, he turned to the Texas &

Pacific man. "You need to get that locomotive turned around and this train ready to roll in short order."

The man frowned at him. "I know who you are. I know you've been made the temporary marshal of this town. But that doesn't give you the right to tell me my business or to decide when trains leave this station or where they go."

Annoyed, Cord produced the letter. He was in no mood to placate men jealous of their own authority. "While you read that, let me explain. This town may soon be attacked by a large body of heavily armed men. You will carry women and children and any others who wish to evacuate back to Fort Worth. Tonight."

"But...but...." The man spluttered indignantly. "That cannot be done without authority..." And then he saw the signature on the letter and fell silent.

Cord heard the clack and clatter of a telegraph key and glanced towards the window. The young man nodded. "Wire is still up, Sir," he confirmed.

Back at the window, Cord dictated a terse message, the telegrapher keying in the Morse code as he listened.

"To Quartermaster U.S. Army Fort Worth. Stop. Women and children evacuating Wolf Creek arrive tonight. Stop. Will need food and shelter. Stop. Contact Colonel Ezariah Bronson Fort Leavenworth. End of message. But I don't want that sent until two hours after the train has departed, understand?"

Cord laid a silver dollar on the window shelf and turned back to the Texas & Pacific man. "Are any other westbound trains scheduled today or tonight?"

"Not until tomorrow afternoon. But we have no passenger cars."

"You have these," said Cord, gesturing at the train that had just rolled in.

Captain Bolt had been standing there, grim, arms folded, watching as Cord took charge. But now he spoke up. "What about the payroll? And my men?"

"I assume your men go where the payroll goes. And as to that, I have a suggestion."

"I bet you do," said Bolt drily.

II.

An hour later two wagons borrowed from Alamo Freight pulled up in front of the Wolf Creek bank, each carrying five soldiers guarding a chest the size of a steamer trunk. An Alamo teamster named Loomis drove the first wagon, and Cord sat beside him. Loomis used every epithet in the book and a few Cord didn't think he had ever heard before to chastise the mules pulling the wagon, even though the knobheads seemed to be doing their job. Cord was glad when the short trip was over, and jumped down off the seat of the first wagon to intercept a perplexed Benjamin Dole as he emerged from the building. He pulled the banker aside as Captain Bolt, who had been riding next to the driver of the second wagon, directed his soldiers to get the chests inside.

"What's going on here?" asked Dole. "What's in those chests?"

"Army payroll, Sir," replied Bolt. "We are commandeering your bank for a while."

"You're what??? But you can't just ...."

He stopped as Cord produced the letter and held it up for him to read. "But we can," he said, amiably. "And we are. Please note the signature at the bottom."

"President Ulysses S. Grant, President, United...." Dole looked up at Cord, flabbergasted. "But you can't just take over a private bank! What about my customers? What about their money?"

"Safer now than they were before," replied Cord, as he heard Bolt order the two drivers to take the wagons back to the train and load up all the sandbags from the flatbed cars. Then Bolt walked over and introduced himself to Dole.

"I would think that the United States Army had the wherewithal to take care of its own business without involving a private enterprise," groused Dole.

Glaring, Bolt replied, "And I would think a private citizen living on the edge of civilization would be happy to do whatever he could for soldiers who played an important role in keeping wild Comanches out of his bank!"

Cord moved away from the two men and scanned the street, curious to see what effect the arrival of two wagon loads of soldiers at the bank had on the local populace. There were knots of people in the street and on the boardwalks, looking his way and talking.

Then he noticed the saloon girl named Kitty standing in front of The Palace watching the goings-on at the bank. That by itself wasn't unusual—it looked like half of Wolf Creek was looking, too. But it was her reaction when she noticed that Cord was watching her. She looked alarmed, and turned to hasten back into the saloon.

Cord crossed the street and entered The Palace, but didn't see her on the main floor. He went back outside and to the corner of the building to peer up Crockett Street—just in time to see Kitty emerge from the alley that ran behind the saloon and turn north, away from him, up Crockett. She wore a brown cloak and as she began to hurry down the boardwalks she pulled the hood up over her head. It was another chilly late autumn day but Cord found himself wondering if that was why Kitty had pulled the hood up. He crossed the street diagonally and followed her from the other side. Then he slowed down and sheltered in a doorway when she, too quartered across Crockett, and turned left at the next intersection. He broke into a run and turned the corner, too. She was heading for edge of town, and the path that led down the slope to the creek, the route he had taken earlier that day to reach Dulcey Garnet's shanty. He doubted that Kitty was visiting whores in the shantytown though.

She was about twenty strides ahead of him when he called her name.

Kitty turned, eyes big as saucers, and stood rooted to the weathered planking of the boardwalk as he closed the distance between them with long strides. When he reached her, he fished the marshal's star out of his pocket, showed it to her, and took her arm firmly with the other hand.

"You're coming with me, Kitty."

"I didn't do anything wrong," she said, and glanced over her shoulder and up at the wooded slope beyond the creek.

"I'm sure you don't think so." Cord looked up at the slope too, silently chiding himself for assuming that the man Dulcey reported seeing in the tree up there was just a hunter getting an eyeful of the half-naked women at the shanties. "But I don't want Arch Cullen to know that the army payroll is in the bank, not on that train. Not just yet."

She glared at him sullenly, and he tightened his grip as he took her back to Milam, and turned towards Front Street and the jail.

They had just turned onto Front and gone past The Palace when Emma came riding up on the high-spirited pinto she had named Longshot. The horse was fiddle-footing and trying to drop its head, trying to take the reins, but Emma sat sublimely relaxed in her black saddle, and handled him like it was nothing at all.

"I was in the round pen at Bohannon's when I heard the train whistle," she told Cord, who thought it was just like his sister to work all day with a horse. "Is it here?"

He nodded. "It is. Finally."

Emma looked curiously at Kitty. "Who is this?"

"The person we've been looking for." He resumed walking towards the jail, dragging the reluctant saloon girl along. Emma held the prancing pinto to a walk and stayed abreast of them, dismounting when they reached their destination, tethering Longshot securely to a hitching post and following her brother and his prisoner inside.

She went inside just in time to see the shocked expression on Toby Jukes' face when Cord came in with Kitty obviously in custody. The young deputy looked blankly at the saloon girl and then at Cord. "What's going on?"

"She's under arrest, Toby. You can be the one to check her for weapons if you want."

Toby looked at Kitty again. "What...what is this all about?"

"Oh for pity's sake!" exclaimed Kitty, exasperated. "I'm sorry, Toby, but you really are dumber than a fence post."

Emma was starting to feel sorry for Toby, who looked like he'd just been poleaxed, so she walked up and got in Kitty's face.

"If you can't say something nice, don't say anything at all—or I'll knock your teeth out." She turned to Toby. "She's Arch Cullen's spy."

"Arch Cullen? But I thought he was in Mexico."

"He was," said Cord. "But he's here now. He's after the army payroll. I believe he is camped in the woods to the northwest of town." He chided himself for dismissing the man Dulcey had seen on the wooded slope as a hunter wanting a glimpse of naked ladies, working on the assumption that Cullen's lookouts would try to keep out of sight. "He may even be close enough to have heard the train whistle earlier. But Kitty here was going to tell him the army payroll had been moved into the bank. Isn't that right, Kitty?"

"That's right," said Kitty, with a sulking glance in Emma's direction. "And he's going to get it, too. He's got a hundred men with him. Some of them rode with him during the War. You see, Arch never stopped fighting that war. He's going to take that payroll and he's going to kill anyone who stands in his way!" She turned her attention to Toby. "You actually thought I was in love with you!" She laughed. "I was just fucking you because I knew if there was advance word on the shipment's arrival you would find out about it, and you would tell me because you have a big mouth and you...."

Emma punched her right in the mouth, and Kitty went down. She sat there, spitting blood as she wept. Rubbing her knuckles, Emma glanced at Toby and said, "You're a nice, good-looking man, and you can do a lot better than this hag."

Toby looked from Kitty to Emma to Cord and by the time his eyes fastened on the latter he looked angry, which Cord thought was the first step to recovering from the shock he had just suffered. "What are the charges, Mr. Remington? I mean, Marshal."

"Accessory to the commission of an armed robbery. That should do."

Toby nodded, grabbed Kitty by the arm and wrenched her none too gently to her feet. "Come on, bitch. You get the cell all by yourself this time."

Smiling a satisfied smile, Emma turned to her brother. "Want me to go up into those woods and find Cullen and his men?"

Cord had no doubt that she could do the job. She could track ants across the desert. "Yes, but you're not going alone."

They heard the loud clang of a cell door being slammed shut, the jingle of keys, and then Toby returned to the office, closing the cellblock door behind him and throwing the ring of keys on the kneehole desk.

"You think Arch Cullen has a hundred men riding with him, Marshal?"

"No. Maybe half as many."

"I sure wish he had stayed in Mexico. He's the last of Quantrill's lieutenants left alive, isn't he?"

Cord nodded. After the raid on Lawrence, William Quantrill had led his guerrillas south into East Texas, but three of his lieutenants—Bloody Bill Anderson, George Todd and Arch Cullen—had split up most of Quantrill's men among themselves and headed back to the border states. Quantrill went to Kentucky with a few faithful followers, was trapped by federal troops and wounded in a shootout, dying from those wounds a few days later. Anderson was shot down in 1864, his corpse dragged through the streets of Richmond, Missouri. Todd, whose group was attached to the army of General Sterling Price, was shot dead in his saddle by a Union sniper.

"According to John Smith," he said, "Cullen and other Confederate leaders want to start a new Confederacy south of the border, but they need a lot of money to do that."

"Smith the storekeeper?" asked Toby, startled. "How would he know?"

"I'll let him tell you."

"We've got to let Mayor Buckley know. The whole town needs to know. Maybe I should send a telegram to the county sheriff in Brownwood. And the Texas Rangers in Waco!"

"You send telegrams like that and Cullen has a man tapping into that line, they'll be shooting up this town in no time. No, we need to buy time to get ready. What I want you to do is go find John Smith. Tell him about Kitty. Tell him the payroll has been moved to the bank. And tell him my sister and I have an idea where Cullen is bivouacked and we're going to go find out exactly how many riders he has. Then go tell Buckley to have the town council assembled in … let's say three hours from now."

Toby nodded. He was ashen-faced. "When do you think he'll come? Cullen, I mean."

"Odds are they'll come in the morning. During the war, he and his kind usually struck at dawn. That gave them all day to put miles between themselves and their crimes. It's hard to keep that many men together after nightfall if you're being chased or you keep moving because you think you might be."

Toby nodded, wondering how it was that Cord Remington, who couldn't be but a few years older than he was, could know so much about how bad men acted. "Well, don't go getting yourself killed, Marshal. Wolf Creek needs you." He glanced at Emma. "You too, Miss."

Emma beamed, and walked over to give the young deputy a peck on the cheek. "That's so sweet. Don't you worry about us."

Toby could only stand there, blushing beet-red and at a loss for words, as the Remingtons walked out.

"Well," said Cord wryly, once he had closed the door behind them. "I think you cured Toby of his infatuation with Kitty."

Emma walked around the tall pinto, took hold of the pommel of her black saddle and vaulted aboard the horse in one fluid, graceful motion with touching boot to stirrup. Then she extended a hand. "Come on. Ride with me to Bohannon's to fetch your horse." She was eager to begin the search for Cullen's camp.

Cord smiled. His sister was a thrill-seeker. She had shown him that back when she performed dangerous horseback stunts at the fairs at which they had made names for themselves. But now it was the risks inherent in the work they did. And he could not think of a bigger risk than riding out to find a camp filled with killers led by one of the war's most notorious and sadistic leaders.

"Not just yet. I have something to see to, first."

"I'll be waiting at the Livery," she said, and then spun the horse around and let it loose to gallop west down Front Street, both rider and horse turning many a head.

Cord walked that way, but before reaching the bridge turned north on Crockett, down the slope to the creek and crossed to the row of shanties. A townsman he knew by sight but not by name was ahead of him, touching the brim of his bowler hat to the several whores who were lounging half-clad in their doorways, but he didn't stop walking. Cord lengthened his stride, and caught up with the man as he reached Dulcey's door and raised a fist to knock. Cord grabbed his arm and spun him around.

"She's not open for business."

"Who says?" asked the townsman, belligerently, and Cord caught a whiff of whiskey emanating from him.

Cord showed him the marshal's badge. "Go find another," he advised, "or you can sober up in a jail cell."

Once the man had moved on to engage another of the girls in conversation, Cord knocked on the door. When Dulcey didn't open it, and he heard no sound from inside, he went in. She was sprawled across the bed, clad in a low-cut corset and lace-trimmed pantaloons. He touched her arm, softly spoke her name, shook her gently—but couldn't rouse her. He bent down, his face close to hers, and caught the scent then, carried on the warm exhalations of breath through her slightly parted lips, that spicy, flowery scent of nutmeg and sassafras and myrrh—and the black poppy. She had taken some laudanum.

Cord sighed, and tried not to think about what the townsman might have done had he been the one to enter the shanty after getting no response to a knock on the door. That was a train of thought he didn't want to travel on, and focused instead on the reason he had come here.

Deciding she might be less trouble passed out than awake but still under the effect of the potion, he packed her trunk with all her belongings, including the bottle of laudanum, and in the process found the greenbacks he had given her. Shoving these in a pocket, he hoisted her over a shoulder, grabbed one handle of the trunk, and kicked the door open to go out.

The other whores stared as he trudged past them. "Ladies, trouble is coming this way, and if you don't care to be shanghaied south of the border to become strumpets of a New Confederacy, I suggest you find a safer place to hide in town, or catch the train that leaves tonight for Fort Worth."

He had managed to transport his burden halfway to the train station, smiling wryly at those who stopped to stare—since it wasn't every day that one saw a woman in her undergarments being carried like he was carrying Dulcey—when he felt the trunk being lifted from the back and turned to see the mulatto girl, dressed in a plain green cotton canvas dress and carrying a carpet bag. She reached down to take the other handle of Dulcey's trunk and he stopped.

"I want to go," she said calmly, and glanced at the unconscious Dulcey. "She has helped me. She is my friend." Her sincerity was genuine, and Cord nodded, which brought a smile to her lips. "My name is Zola."

"Let's get moving then. It's not much further."

When they reached the station there were thirty or so women and children on the platform, as well as a dozen or so armed townsmen. Cord and Zola put down the trunk and he gently eased Dulcey onto it, sitting up with her back against the wall. Zola sat beside her, an arm around her, and Dulcey's head slumped onto the mulatto's shoulder. Cord. pressed two fingers against the side of her neck and felt her pulse. It was slow and strong.

Cord went inside the station and found the Texas & Pacific man he had spoken to before. This time the railroad man was more amenable. He informed Cord that the T&PRR was providing free passage for those who wished to leave Wolf Creek that evening.

Returning to Dulcey, he helped Zola put a dress on her, over the garments she was already wearing. He was aware of the looks some of the people on the platform were giving them. A mother hurried her young son past, hiding his eyes while giving Cord a very disapproving stare. Bringing a woman of ill-repute to the station in her undergarments was no doubt outrageous, but he had little time or patience for propriety.

Once Dulcey was dressed Cord had made up his mind. He gave the roll of greenbacks he had initially given Dulcey to the mulatto then added another hundred dollars.

"The train won't leave for a couple of hours yet. I can't stay with her. This is enough to get both of you to Santa Fe. That is, if you will agree to take her there."

"I will take her there. But I have money."

"Just the same, take this. I will pay you this much again for doing this for me. Once you get to Santa Fe ask anyone how for directions to La Fonda. That's a hotel. I live there. When you get there ask at the desk for a man named Quintero. He will take care of you both until I get back."

Zola pushed the roll of bills under the bodice of her dress, between her breasts. "You can count on me," she said earnestly.

"I believe I can." Cord brushed a stray tendril of tousled golden hair out of Dulcey's face, then left the platform and bent his steps for Bohannon's, relieved that at least Dulcey Garnet and her friend would be spared the hell that was coming to Wolf Creek.

CHAPTER EIGHT

The Coming Storm

I.

When Cord arrived at the livery, Emma was still on Longshot, training him to back up, while Ned Bohannon was over in the shade of the smitty's ramada, sitting on his three-legged stool, slumped back against an old post, snoring. There was an uncorked jug on the ground and the livery owner's finger was still curled through the handle. His son, Win, was over at the stalls, but when he saw the Remingtons he came running. Cord's long-legged bay was in the in the speckled shade of the dusty elms in a corral adjacent to the roofed, three-sided smitty. The dark bay had spotted him as well, and was coming up to the railing, whickering and tossing its black mane.

"Afternoon, Marshal!" said Win, excited to have company. Then he looked at Emma as she swung down off the pinto, which was still nodding prancing, clearly unhappy to no longer be in motion. "Afternoon, Miss," he murmured, his cheeks turning ruddy even before she swung her cool, emerald gaze in his direction.

"Good afternoon to you, Win. I swear you are more handsome now than you were this morning."

Win fidgeted in place, kicking at dust, the compliment plunging him into a perfect torment of giddy embarrassment. "I, um … I …"

Coming to the boy's rescue, Cord said, "I need my horse saddled, Win, if you don't mind."

"Yes, Sir!" squeaked Win and ran off.

Cord's gaze swept from one end of the livery to the other, his smile quickly fading. It occurred to him that Cullen would likely come for the horses here. Many horses and mules had been slaughtered by Quantrill's men at Lawrence, and most of those left alive were carried off by the raiders. This was because the Border War had been largely fought by mounted units, so horses were always in demand. Here in Wolf Creek, Cullen might want spare mounts for his men, or he might just want to scatter the horses in town to discourage immediate pursuit. Either way, Cord had to accept that Bohannon's enterprise was a likely target.

When he shared his thoughts with Emma he added, "I overheard someone saying that Ned here was a mountain man back in the Thirties, and later on a buffalo hunter...."

"Yes, well, he's an old drunk now," said Emma, none too kindly, remembering Bohannon's comments about women when she and Cord had first arrived in Wolf Creek. She was not one to forgive or forget.

"I was going to say, even if he still could shoot the knots out of a plank at a hundred yards I don't think he could protect himself and his son from Cullen's killers."

"Well. I can't be down here when the shooting starts, and you can't, either," she said. "So why don't we just do the old curmudgeon a favor and run the horses off tonight. Without horses, who would bother with this old place—or this old man?"

"And what about our horses when the attack comes?"

Emma thought it over. "The Alamo Freight yard. Thick adobe wall all the way around." She looked at her brother, and could see he was expecting something more. "Alright, I'll talk to the owner over there, and see if he will take Bohannon's horses."

When Win arrived with his horse, Cord climbed into the saddle and gave the boy a silver dollar. Then the boy got the mesquite pole gate for them, and watched the Remingtons cross the bridge and turn north on Crockett towards the wooded hills.

Cord couldn't help glancing at the row of shanties when they reached the creek. A couple of the whores, half-clad, were sharing a fire, and he heard one of them burst into bawdy laughter. Apparently, they had not taken his warning about the coming storm too seriously. He shook his head and urged the responsive bay across the creek where the rock crossing had been created. Looking up at the wooded slope above him he tried to put Dulcey Garnet out of his mind and focus on the dangerous task ahead.

His horse, having been cooped up in a livery stall or pen for several days, was aching to run, trying to take the reins, but Cord held it in check. He wasn't in the saddle to go galloping headlong into the trees in search of the enemy. He was on horseback in case he had to ride hell-bent for leather out of them.

Unlike his sister, Cord didn't name his mounts. But of all that he had ridden in his time, this one was his favorite. The gelding's lineage ran back into the late 1700's in the Carolinas, and in Tennessee in Andrew Jackson's time. Emma's new horse looked like he could run from sunup to sundown, but Cord thought his bay, with its thoroughbred roots, could beat Longshot in a short race.

The day was becoming overcast, gray-bellied clouds moving doggedly across the sky from the north-northwest. Cord pulled the collar of his long-coat up, glanced across at Emma. She was scanning the slope with the eyes of a hawk, and she seemed impervious to the weather. He had met some brave and stalwart men—men you could count on to stand with you through hell and high water. But he couldn't think of anyone better than his own sister to have at his side at a time like this.

On the north side of the creek, a trail led along the creek embankment. He had to wonder if Cullen had a man—or more—up there at the top of the hill, watching anyone who came from or went to town. It would be a perfect vantage point, where someone could see Wolf Creek from one end to the other. And he be able to see a large body of men coming out of town and across the creek—a sure sign that the presence of Cullen's bunch had been discovered. The big question was what he would think of a man and a woman holding their horses to a walk as they rode along the base of the hill, heading west. But Cord had been unable to come up with a better option. Waiting until night to try to sneak across the creek and up the slope to find a lookout in the dark and avoid any gunfire that might alert the camp they were trying to sneak up on wasn't very likely.

About a quarter of a mile further on, another trail branched off the first, leading up a wash that was crisscrossed with roots and rocks that made it look like a natural staircase leading deeper into the woods. Before he turned up that trail, Cord twisted in the saddle and looked behind him. If there was a lookout, and if he stood anywhere near the best spot to see what was going on in town, then he and Emma had moved out of sight, and by turning to go up the steep slope along the wash, were circling round that high lookout point.

The thick woods closed quickly round them as they kept climbing. The going soon became so steep they had to dismount and lead their horses. The winter wind gamboled in the top of the live oaks, sassafras and mulberry trees, but otherwise it was very quiet. There were no birds singing; Cord put that down to the changing weather. The underbrush was pretty dense in places and he realized chances were poor of spotting a sentry or sniper, if one or more had been posted around the camp. Frequently they stopped and listened and peered through the brush. The temperature was dropping, and their exhalations were vapor in the frigid air.

When they reached the top of the slope they stayed on foot to make smaller targets. Eventually Emma stopped and whispered, "We're veering off to the east a bit. The town is over my right shoulder now." Cord nodded. He didn't question his sister's infallible sense of direction. They began moving north again.

Longshot noticed it first. The paint picked up his head sharply and whickered. Cord smelled it then. Wood smoke. The ground began sloping downward, and they came to a trail which had been traveled recently by horsemen. They followed the trail briefly, until Emma grabbed his sleeve and pointed at the ground—recently horses had veered off to the right, between two hillocks where the underbrush was sparse. Following the tracks about thirty yards, they stopped again. The smell of smoke was stronger now. They tied up their horses, and Emma made a mental note to get started on training Longshot to stand ground-hitched. In situations such as this she didn't like tying her horse, preferring him free to come running at her signal, a short-long sequence of whistles. That part would take some time but she had confidence in the pinto.

Taking the Winchester 1873 out of its saddle boot, and a spyglass out of the pannier tied to her saddle, Emma headed north, slowly making her way through the forest's underlying brush, Cord followed. He had chosen not to take the time to retrieve his Spencer rifle from the Longhorn Hotel. She didn't think anything of it. Long-range shooting was her forte, not his. He was better suited for close-in work. Though not a quick-draw artist, he seldom missed a pistol shot. Then there were his custom-made knives. And if all else failed, his fists were weapons by their own right.

The terrain was gently rolling, and sloping downward. They had gone maybe a hundred feet when they spotted several plumes of wood smoke drifting up through the trees about fifty yards up ahead. But they couldn't see the light of the fires or any part of a camp so they assumed it was located out of sight down in a ravine or hollow.

Emma got down on one knee behind the trunk of a large oak and laid the One in One Thousand rifle on the ground, pulled the spyglass from her belt and opened it slowly. It was a safe bet that Cullen would have sentries posted, and it would be very useful to be able to locate the one—or more—who were posted here, south of the camp. Using the spyglass, she thoroughly scanned the woods, starting to her left. Her task was not made any easier by the darkening of the day as winter clouds thickened.

It didn't take her long. She saw the shape of a man separate itself from the thick trunk of an old mulberry tree about sixty feet away, to the east, and a moment later discovered why—he didn't want to relieve himself in the same spot where he was standing watch. Emma pointed him out to Cord, then spent a few more minutes thoroughly scanning the brush to the west and behind them to the south, then closed the spyglass, glanced at her brother and shook her head. She was pretty sure an experienced guerrilla fighter like Arch Cullen would have more than one sentry posted on this side of his camp, but she couldn't find any more.

Cord watched the spot where the sentry, now that he had relieved himself, stepped back into the brush growing around the trunk of the mulberry. He realized that he and Emma were lucky to have avoided detection thus far. As long as there was a chance they could find out what they needed to know—how many men rode with Cullen—without being discovered, then taking out the sentry wasn't an option. If anything happened to one of the sentries it would alert Cullen to the fact that he and his men had been located. How he would react to that knowledge was the terrible unknown. Would he ride down into Wolf Creek right then and there? While the payroll shipment was in the bank building and Bolt and his detail were settling in to defend it, there was no guarantee that the captain and his men could hold Cullen at bay, while the townspeople, with the exceptions of John Smith and Toby Jukes, were blissfully unaware of the terrible danger that lurked in these dark woods.

He gestured for Emma to head westward, and to do so slowly. They needed to move laterally around the camp's location until they could find a better place to get closer—or, preferably, higher. Emma nodded, picked up her rifle, and headed west in a deep crouch, using the underbrush to the best possible advantage.

They hadn't gone far before spotting the trunk of a tall tree that had fallen in the downhill direction and been caught up in the limbs of a stout live oak. The trunk was slanted at about a thirty-degree angle. There were branches and stubs that were all that remained of limbs sprouted from the trunk about fifteen feet up from the exposed roots. Cord thought it possible that if he shimmied up that trunk he could elevate himself enough to look down into the enemy camp and get a head count. The one problem was that if there was a sentry nearby he would probably be seen going up the trunk. But he felt like he was running out of time. He had to take the chance.

When he gestured to Emma that he was going up the tree she shook her head.

"I weigh less," she whispered. "And I've always been the better climber."

"This tree is plenty strong to hold me." He held out a hand.

Emma frowned, but laid the spyglass in his hand.

Cord began his agile ascent up the slanted tree trunk. He made good time, with plenty of hand and foot holds, and limber enough to get around or under brittle dead branches that might give him away if he blundered and snapped them. Twenty-five feet off the ground he came to a shattered limb nearly as thick as the trunk at that point, sticking straight up about four feet. He lay down on the trunk, one foot braced against a conveniently located stub, and wrapped his left arm round the limb. From this vantage point he looked north and down through the limbs of the oak tree, which had been stripped of most of its leaves by the persistent north wind, and into a wide ravine.

Cullen's camp was there.

Three blazing campfires were producing plenty of wood smoke being blown southward by the prevailing wind, with men gathered round them, and more men roaming through the camp or standing and talking. Beyond the fires were several picket lines, and Cord counted the horses. There were forty-four of them, and seven mules no doubt used for packing supplies. This wasn't just an outlaw gang, it was a company of hardcase killers. Then he saw something that made him break out the spyglass.

At the east end of the camp was a canvas tarpaulin secured to four saplings, sheltering a folding table. Three men stood on one side of the table, looking down at what appeared to be, by its size, a map. A fourth man, on the opposite side of the table from the others, was leaning over, tapping the map there, and there, and another place. Cord wondered if the map was of Wolf Creek and, further, whether it had been supplied by Kitty. It was being curled at the corners by the wind whipping up, but held in place by the weight of a S&W 1871 Russian Model, regarded by many to be the most accurate pistol made.

Cord didn't have to wonder about the identity of the fourth man. It wasn't just the way he was using the map. It was the deference with which the other three men stood there watching and listening. Their body language informed him that the fourth man was the leader of this pack.

Arch Cullen was a slender man of medium height, with long lank straw-colored hair curled back behind his ears, beneath a Kossuth hat pulled low over his angular, gaunt-cheeked face. When he straightened up and hooked his thumbs under his belt, this pushed back his faded canvas duster enough for Cord to put the spyglass on the gun rig around his waist. The holster was empty. So the Smith & Wesson Russian belonged to him. It was a shootist's gun.

Laying eyes on The Angel of Death for the first time, Cord's thoughts turned to John Smith's harrowing account of what this man had done to his mother and father. He thought about the sixteen soldiers who had been killed in the taking of the first payroll shipment. And he thought about all the people down in Wolf Creek whose lives were in danger. He found himself contemplating putting a bullet through Cullen's head right then and there. It was something he had never done before, a cold-blooded assassination. That would be doing the world a favor, and probably save many lives in the long run. Thou not necessarily the lives of the people of Wolf Creek. But he didn't have his carbine and he wasn't going to ask Emma to kill in cold blood, and the chances that he and his sister could get out of these woods alive were slim and none if such a shot was made.

Having seen all he needed to see, Cord made his way back down the tree. He was turning to Emma, expecting her to ask him how many heads or horses he had counted when a gruff voice came from behind her and his gaze swung to the man who stepped out from behind a tree, a pistol in each hand.

"You all shed your shootin' irons, and move real slow, 'less you want to die, right here, right now."

Emma's eyes flashed wide with surprise as she looked at Cord. Her Winchester was racked over her shoulder, and he knew what her first thought was, to roll and come up shooting with the long gun, but he shook his head once, even as his hand came up closer to the Schofield riding on his right hip, under the longcoat. He was debating whether to push Emma aside and trade lead with the man behind her—until another man spoke up, this one behind him.

"Bob said real slow, mister." The double-click of a hammer being thumbed back punctuated his menacing reminder.

Emma tossed the Winchester off to the right. Cord slowly pulled his Schofield revolver out of its holster and tossed it to his left.

"Will you look at that, Joe," said Bob. "This woman's wearin' pants."

"A woman's got no call wearin' pants," said Joe. "We best get 'em off her."

Bob chuckled. "We're going to have a party in camp tonight!"

Emma sobbed and turned to throw herself into Cord's arms. In doing so, she slipped her arms under his longcoat.

"Don't you worry, mister," sneered Joe. "We'll let you watch your woman entertain us for a while...'fore we kill you." He was circling round to Cord's right, intent on picking up the discarded pistol and rifle.

"Let's get one thing straight," said Cord. "She's not 'my woman'. She's my sister."

"Well, whatever she is, I hope she lasts until daylight anyways," said Bob. "We got lots of friends down there in that camp you was spying on. Now you let go of her so's she can get shed those pants. It riles me seein' a woman wearing pants."

"Don't you want to know why we were spying on your camp?" asked Cord.

Bob looked across at Joe, and Joe looked back at Bob, and then they shrugged in unison.

"You want to know, Bob?" asked Joe.

"Nope. Don't much matter anyway."

Cord felt Emma's hand close around the handle of the knife on his left hip.

"Awright now, girly," said Bob. "Turn around and...."

Emma whirled, throwing the knife side-arm. It was suddenly sprouting from Bob's chest; the blade having passed between two of his ribs to pierce his heart. He was still standing when he died. His corpse began to tilt sideways.

Before it could hit the ground Cord was turning to face Joe, who was staring at what had once been Bob and wondering what had happened to him. Reaching back under his longcoat, Cord whipped the second knife out of the sheath on his right hip. Joe was now standing six feet to his right, looming over the discarded Schofield. His eyes swung away from Bob and met Cord's in the instant that Cord closed the gap between them in a single stride and slashed right through the veins and tendons on the inside of his right wrist. The pistol was slipping from useless fingers when Cord took another step, reaching out to grab Joe by the front of his shirt with his left hand while plunging the razor-sharp double blade of the knife to the hilt into his temple. Like Bob, Joe was dead before he hit the ground, brief spurting fountains of blood issuing from both wrist and temple.

Emma picked up her rifle while Cord retrieved his pistol and holstered it before bending down again to wipe the knife blade clean using Joe's shirt. Then he walked over to Bob, sat on his heels and pulled the knife Emma had thrown out of the dead man's chest and cleaned it in a similar fashion. He glanced at his sister.

"I didn't know you could throw a blade like that."

Emma shrugged. "I learned by watching you. I had the best seat in the house, remember? The first few times you performed with knives in public I was the one with her back to the wall praying you didn't get a speck of dust in your eye."

"That's right. Now I remember." Cord sheathed his knives as he stood up, then grabbed Bob by the bootheels and dragged him into the nearest brush. He did the same with Joe. He was standing there looking down at the two dead men without the slightest remorse. They had been bad men through and through, and deserved killing. But eventually they would be missed. He was hoping it wouldn't be until sundown, preferably later. He was fairly certain Arch Cullen wouldn't ride into Wolf Creek at night.

Emma touched his arm. "We had better get going. There isn't much daylight left."

She led the way, and he kept an eye on their backtrail. By the time they got back to the horses, snow was drifting down from the wind-thrashed canopy of the trees. When they reached town it was snowing and dusk had come early.

II.

Wolf Creek didn't have a town hall, so the council meeting took place in a back room of The Palace Saloon & Gaming Emporium. Colonel Buckley, the establishment's owner, called it the Red Room and when he first stepped inside Cord understood why. A side door facing Houston Street allowed people to enter the room without passing through the saloon, and when he and

Emma went through that door the first thing Cord noticed was the red damask on the walls and a blood-red Oriental rug beneath the long mahogany table that was the room's centerpiece. Through an interior door came the sounds of the saloon beyond, men talking, women laughing, a piano being played.

There were six men in the room. Toby Jukes stood self-consciously at one end of the table, looking greatly relieved to see the Remingtons. Colonel Buckley was pacing up and down the room like a wild animal caught in a cage. Alamo Freight's Jack Jacoby, a tall, florid, redheaded man, stood with feet planted well apart and arms folded, glowering at the floor. Benjamin Dole, the president of the bank, sat at the table with Amos Chelico, owner of the Continental Cafe.

The sixth man was John Smith. He too was sitting at the table, looking impatient. As soon as Cord walked in he could tell that the Pinkerton man had told the council members about Arch Cullen.

"For the love of God, Mr. Remington," said Col. Buckley, "tell us it isn't true."

Every pair of eyes followed Cord as he crossed the room to the big stone hearth where a fire was blazing. He was frozen clean through. "It's true," he said. "Arch Cullen is camped north of town with about forty men."

"Forty men!" exclaimed Jacoby. "Are you sure about that?"

"Well, there *were* forty-four saddle horses," remarked Emma as she leaned over the table and examined the label of each of the four bottles on a large silver tray which also contained clean glasses. She poured herself a generous dollop of Old Overholt whiskey and drank it down like a sailor, much to the amusement of her brother and the amazement of the others in the room. "But Cullen has two less men than he did yesterday."

The members of the town council exchanged looks. Emma's tone was so carefree that Jacoby had to ask, "You mean...you killed two of his men."

"We found their camp," said Emma, matter-of-factly, as she plopped wearily into a chair next to Smith. "A couple of sentries spotted us. They won't be coming to town tomorrow. But I would be willing to bet that the rest of them will, eager to do some robbing and killing and such."

"And you're sure it's that devil Cullen leading them?" asked Dole. The banker was wringing his hands, obviously in a high state of anxiety.

Smith banged a fist on the table. "God damn it, I've told you, that bastard Cullen is the leader. Why don't you believe me?"

"It's not that we don't believe you, really," said Chelico calmly. He smiled wistfully "We just don't want to."

"You can be damn sure that every man who rides with Cullen is a killer," said Smith. "A good many are probably Missouri men, like Cullen himself. Border Ruffians. Those people will never stop fighting that damned war. And I have already told you what they do when they raid a town. The only question now is what you men are prepared to do about it."

There was moment of stunned silence as the council members exchange looks. Then Benjamin Dole, looking quite distraught, spoke up, his high-pitched voice pitched higher than usual.

"I don't understand why they had to put the army payroll in my bank."

"Because it's the only structure in Wolf Creek that I've seen that can't be burned down," said Cord.

"We can't let them burn any building down," said Buckley. "Not in our town. I'll tell you how we handle this. We have probably sixty able-bodied men who can fight. Some were in the war. We'll stand up to these marauders. We will stand together to meet them head-on. And as God is my witness, we'll drive them off."

Cord moved to the head of the table, planted the knuckles of both hands on the polished mahogany surface and looked from one council member to the next as he spoke.

"Most of you don't know me and my sister. We were contracted by the United States government to make sure the payroll shipment currently in your local bank was not stolen, and to stop the men who stole the one a couple of months ago, killing every soldier in the detail that was guarding that shipment. I carry a letter signed by President Grant. But I don't think I need that letter to persuade you to listen to me. I have a plan. I cannot guarantee that this plan will save every Wolf Creek citizen's life. But I do believe it's our only chance to save this town and stop Arch Cullen once and for all. The question is—do you want to hear it?"

Jacoby nodded. "I want to hear it, Mr. Remington."

"I'll listen" said Chelico.

Buckley nodded. Dole just sat there looking miserable.

"Colonel, you will *not* gather together the men of Wolf Creek and stand your ground against the likes of these raiders. Yes, every man should arm himself. Mr. Smith has rifles and ammunition available for those who need them. But the men will fight to defend the *town*, not the bank, not the payroll. You leave that to the army, and to my sister and myself.

"Starting right away, and working through the night if necessary, we need to get everything that will carry water, from casks to buckets to cooking utensils and laundry tubs and even canteens and fill them up. Drain every well. Make as many trips to the creek as is needed. Every building should have as much water as possible stored inside."

"I have rolls of canvas which can be used to line barrels and casks that should then hold water," said Smith.

"I have a half-dozen cider barrels right here at The Palace that will hold thirty-two gallons of water. And a dozen or more casks," said Buckley.

"Colonel, you should take charge of the water," suggested Cord. "Don't forget to check with Wong Li. He had a lot of containers, including bathtubs. Every window should be boarded up. If there are empty houses, get the timber from them. Mr. Chelico, if you don't mind managing that...."

"I will do my best, Sir," said the Continental's owner.

"If someone throws a torch or anything else that's burning into a building, use the water to put the fire out immediately. If a raider comes through a door or window, then the man or men inside must do their best to kill him. But they should not go out into the street and try to fight the enemy there. They will almost surely die. You can be sure that Cullen's men are ruthless—and very, very good pistoleers.

"Mr. Jacoby, we'll need some of your biggest wagons—and bravest drivers. Emma will explain where and when they'll be needed."

"We'll do our part," said Jacoby. "You can rely on that."

Cord nodded. "I know you will." He looked to John Smith. "Is there anything else?"

"Yes," said the Pinkerton man. "Women should not be left alone. They could be badly used or carried off—or both."

"What about me?" asked Toby Jukes.

"I have a big task for you, Toby," replied Cord. "I want you to ride for the Double D ranch while there's still light. Tell Tom Dundee everything. Tell him that I need him to bring every able-bodied cowboy first thing in the morning. Tell him ... that there's another Two Toes on the loose."

The young deputy looked mystified by the last sentence. Dundee had never regaled him with the story of the hunt for the infamous man-killing cougar. But he nodded. "Yes, Sir, you can count on me. I'll go right now."

Cord glanced at his sister. "You have anything to add, Emma?"

Emma rose and poured eight glasses of Old Overholt. She handed one to Buckley, Jacoby, Chelico and Dole. Then she gave one to Jukes, to John Smith and to her brother, keeping one for herself. There was something about her fetching smile, her confident demeanor, and the way her supple body moved that captivated them all. It was a moment of gentility and grace that had all those present entertaining the hope that order would overcome chaos, that good would triumph over evil. It was a hope that soothed the nerves—of all but Benjamin Dole the banker.

She held her glass high. "With a little luck, tomorrow we'll save Wolf Creek from destruction, protect the army's payroll, and finally put an end to the career of The Angel of Death."

"Hear, hear," said Buckley.

"I'll drink to that," said Smith.

III.

After the meeting in the Red Room had concluded, Emma pulled Jacoby aside and gave him details of the plan she and Cord had hatched on the way back from their reconnoiter of the woods, or that part of the plan that called for eight wagons and how many men and mule teams were needed to move each in place when the time came. From the Palace it was a simple matter to walk up and down Front Street and then up and down Crockett, less than a block in each direction, so she could point out the exact locations she had in mind. Jacoby listened carefully and at the end assured her the wagons would be in place before dawn

That done Emma asked the Alamo Freight Company owner if he and his employees could defend their walled compound located at the east end of Front when the raid came. Jacoby was confident that they could. The compound was enclosed in an adobe wall too high to jump on horseback, and two arched entrances with thick iron-braced wooden gates. Emma inquired if he would try to talk Ned Bohannon into joining him there, with his son Win, and with the horses from the Livery. Jacoby assured her he would accomplish that, one way or the other.

"I have one more question for you," she said. "Would you take my horse and my brother's into your keeping?"

"Of course," said Jacoby, smiling warmly. As he was an adult male with a heartbeat, he was greatly attracted to Emma. "You have my word they will be safe and sound."

"I would be so very grateful."

There was something about the smile she gave him then that made John Jacoby wonder what form her gratitude would take.

Walking to the general store brought Emma close to the middle of town, the intersection of Front Street, running east and west, and Crockett, running north and south. The Palace Saloon was on the northeast corner. The Longhorn Hotel was on the northwest. On the southwest corner was the bank. Blue-coated soldiers were busy stacking sandbags to form a redoubt across the front of the bank. Others were blocking the alley that ran behind the bank with another redoubt, since the bank had a back door.

Wagons were moving in both directions on Front Street, employed in carrying people and sundry items from pails to barrels that could hold water to and from the creek, which they reached using a footpath alongside the bridge at the western end of Front. From all points came the sounds of hammers and saws as a few structures were dismantled so that others could be fortified.

Meanwhile, a few doors down from The Palace, John Smith's store saw a steady stream of men and women coming in empty handed and going out loaded up with pistols, rifles and ammunition Every bucket and pail and cooking utensil that could hold water was already gone. When Emma walked in she found Smith standing in the middle of the store, with the crates that had carried the rifles and guns at his feet.

Emma recalled from her previous visit that there had been four shotguns and five rifles, along with a half-dozen pistols, in a gun cabinet behind the main counter. That cabinet was empty now. Taking off her duster, she pitched in to help Smith. When he gave away a firearm she made sure its new owner got the right ammunition.

A couple of hours after sundown they were done. The only weapons left in the general store were the greener Smith kept loaded and stashed behind the counter and the pistol in his room. Amos Chelico had sent two men with lumber to board up the store's big plate glass window. Smith got a cup of coffee from the potbelly stove in the corner and stood outside the front door with Emma. The hammering was still going on here and there, and the water wagon was still operating. The defenses around the bank appeared to be complete. For a few moments they just stood there, without speaking, listening to Wolf Creek prepare for battle.

"You know your way around guns," said Smith. "If you ever want to dabble in gunrunning...."

He was joking, she could tell. "When I found out I couldn't miss unless there was a problem with the weapon or the ammunition, I began to educate myself."

A shadowy figure was striding towards them on the boardwalk from the direction of The Palace. Smith put a hand on the pistol stuck in his belt but she touched his arm.

"It's Cord," she said.

Smith saw that this was so a moment later when Cord was close enough that light from the lantern next to the mercantile's door illuminated his face. In fact, he looked up at the lantern, curiously.

"You put that up today, didn't you?" he asked Smith.

"That I did. To discourage people from breaking into my store."

"Remember to take it down or empty it before morning. We're ready at the bank. I'm going to try to get a few hours' sleep." He looked to Emma. "You should do the same."

"I will."

Cord looked from her to Smith with a faint smile. He started to turn away, then looked again at the gunrunner-turned-storekeeper.

"You're a gambling man. If you were betting on whether we win the day tomorrow would you raise or fold?"

Smith didn't hesitate. "I would be all in."

Cord nodded and grinned. "The only way to be. Good night, you two." He merged into the night shadows, heading for the Longhorn.

"And he will actually be able to sleep, too," said Emma, enviously.

Smith was gazing at her profile, feeling a stirring in his loins at the closeness of this shockingly beautiful young woman, and gulped down the rest of his coffee. "I think it's about time I tried to do the same. You should try, too."

Emma turned, that fetching, sultry smile on her lips, her eyes smoky and needful. "Are you sure that's what you want me to do?" Boldly, she draped her arms languorously around his neck and leaned her eager, supple body into him. Any notion of doing the right and proper thing abandoned Smith, and he wrapped his arms around her and planted a hard and hungry kiss on her lips that left her breathless, before sweeping her up in his arms and carrying her inside the general store, kicking the door shut behind them.

CHAPTER NINE

The Raid

I.

As expected, Arch Cullen and his raiders came riding into town at daybreak.

It had snowed lightly during the night, leaving the ground and rooftops with a thin layer of white. As the sun peeked over the eastern horizon the world was hushed. No birds sang. No wind blew. It was a hush that often followed on the heels of snowfall, a silence suddenly broken by a cacophony of sounds from the wooded slope to the north of town—the shouts of men, the whinny and snort of horses, as forty men rode pell-mell down that slope, through the brush and young trees, many of them carrying torches.

As the riders reached the bottom of the hill, ten of them crossed the creek where it turned to the west. This brought them near the row of shanties. Two men veered that way while the others rode hard for the bridge that crossed the creek a little further up. Three whores stood outside, wrapped up in blankets against the cold. One of them cast aside her blanket and ran into the creek until the current was strong enough to carry her off. The others ran into two different shanties. One of the raiders made a running dismount and barreled right through the door of one of the shanties, splintering it. The other raider dismounted, too, but kicked the door open and tossed his torch inside. A woman's blood-curdling scream rent the morning and an instant later the whore ran out, engulfed in flames. The raider shot her in the back, caught up his horse and rode on. A moment later the first man emerged from the other shanty, pulling up his trousers and hooking suspenders onto his shoulders. He too mounted up and galloped. By this time flames were consuming the shanty whose resident had been set on fire.

The main body of raiders, led by Arch Cullen, had reached the train tracks and station by then. The latter was locked up tight. They had not expected to find the train there; Cullen was aware that the train had gone east in the night, and correctly assumed it carried evacuating townspeople but not the payroll itself. There wasn't a soul in sight. He shouted to his men that when they found the bluecoats they would find the money, and ordered one of his lieutenants to take half of the thirty riders and circle around to come in from the east, while he led the rest galloping north up Milam Street towards the middle of town. Several men hurled their torches at the station, setting it ablaze.

The ten who had branched off and crossed the creek, reached the bridge to the west of town and paused. To a man they gave Bohannon's Livery a long look, but it became evident that not a person nor horse nor animal of any kind was there. The raiders kicked their milling mounts into a headlong gallop across the bridge and thundered towards the center of town, pistols drawn now, shooting to left and right, though there was no one to shoot at. Glass panes in boarded up windows shattered. Bullets plunked into timber. Then they began taking return fire, rifle and shotgun barrels poked out through those broken windows, spouting flame, noise, and hot lead from between the boards that had been nailed up primarily to prevent riders and torches from coming through.

"Burn 'em out!" shouted one of the raiders, as the mounted men began milling around in the street, shooting and shouting to each other through the din of gunfire. Several torches bounced off the front walls of the buildings, or the wood nailed up at the windows. In one of these cases, a man emerged from a door, bucket in hand, and threw water on the torch—an instant before he was riddled with bullets, performing a jerky dance on the boardwalk, like a puppet subjected to the whimsy of a spastic puppeteer. A structure across the street, housing a barber shop, began to burn, the hungry flames crawling up one corner and then, melting the snow that had gathered on the roof of the porch so that it dripped like rain between the slanted planks wetting the boardwalk enough to turn back the blaze, so that it leaped straight up the front and onto the roof. There were two townsmen in this building, and they fled out the back, coughing and with eyes burning from the smoke that had gathered inside, having seen what had befallen the man who had ventured out to douse a torch and save a building across the street. But several of Cullen's hardcases had already filtered down through the alleys, and both men were gunned down as soon as they emerged.

The riders coming down Front Street from the east, fifteen in number, were greeted by a volley of fire from men behind the high adobe walls of the Alamo Freight Company. During the night, a makeshift parapet had been constructed out of timber on the front walls, and four of John Jacoby's employees, aided by Ned Bohannon and Jacoby himself—three on either side of the gate—began shooting at them, emptying several saddles immediately. A withering return fire commenced. One of the Alamo Freight teamsters toppled off the parapet with a hole in his forehead, dead before he hit the ground, and startling Win Bohannon, who was standing down below. Several torches were thrown at the closed gate. The two men on either side of the wall put down their guns and proceeded to sluice buckets of water onto the front of the gate from above. One of these was Ned Bohannon. They threw the empty buckets to the ground and Win retrieved them, ran to the nearby well and filled them up, then hurried back hauling two at a time, before carrying one at a time up the ladders on either side.

The raiders soon realized they were not going to be able to burn down the gate and get to the horses inside, horses that were packed into Jacoby's two corrals, mulling about excitedly, whinnying and snorting at the din of gunfire and the shouts of men. Their leader led the way towards the center of town. Ned Bohannon rose up and drew a bead on the last rider, squeezing off a shot with his old Hawken Plains rifle that punched the raider out of the saddle. The man riding near him twisted in his saddle and got off a pistol shot that was so notable due to range and circumstances that it would be attributed to Arch Cullen himself. The bullet caught Ned in the cheek and at that angle lodged in his brain. He toppled backwards and was lying dead on the parapet when Win had clambered up the ladder to throw himself, sobbing, across the corpse of his father.

But Arch Cullen was leading the other fifteen Ruffians up Crockett, but they weren't rushing like the two groups riding in from east and west. They took their time, shooting up the buildings and throwing all their torches. It was a well-known fact that clapboard buildings in the west usually went up in flames in no time at all, and Cullen had hoped to have rendered Wolf Creek into a blazing inferno within minutes. But defenders were dousing torches that landed on the boardwalks in front by pitching buckets of water through the slanting boards that crisscrossed windows and some doors, and the snow melting off the roofs aided them. Some of his men rode down the alleys trying to hurl torches up onto the flat rooftops.

Meanwhile Cullen and one of his most trusted men rode closer to the intersection of Crockett and Front, oblivious to the whine and buzz of bullets in the air, and noted the redoubt of sandbags constructed in front of the bank on the other side of Front, with blue-coated soldiers sheltering behind them. This confirmed what he had suspected was the case since being informed of the eastbound train's departure – that the army payroll was kept in the local bank. He grinned wolfishly, hearing the gunfire coming from both ends of Front Street. His intention had been for the eastern and western prongs of his attack to meet him and the balance of his bloodthirsty little army in the center of Wolf Creek. Turning in his saddle, he looked down the street at his men sending a hail of lead into the buildings on both sides of Crockett. Most of his men preferred pistols to rifles, and many carried a dozen or more loaded cylinders for quick reloading, a tactic he had learned from his mentor, Quantrill.

He called his men forward and when they were gathered he pointed at the bank.

"There. The money we need to make our home, a new Confederacy, south of the border. It's in there. If we fail we might as well be dead! But we will NOT fail!" he drew his pistols. "Kill the bluecoats. Kill them all. KILL EVERYTHING!"

He kicked his horse into a lope and his men, their hoarse cheers rising above the din of battle, followed him.

II.

John Smith was at the plate glass window of his general store as Cullen's hellions galloped up Front Street from the east. He hadn't waited for the glass to be shot out, but used the butt of his greener to smash it, so that as the raiders streamed past he could stick the double barrels out between some of the scrap timber that crisscrossed the window. He fired both barrels and was gratified as, squinting through a drift of gunsmoke saw one of the horsemen blown sideways out of his saddle. Breaking open the sawed-off shotgun, he plucked out the empty shell casings and loaded two more 12-gauge cartridges, half-crouching as bullets began to strike the wood which provided him with at least some shelter.

Pushing the barrel through again, he glimpsed two of the raiders on pivoting horses, peppering his location with their pistols. He cut loose with both barrels again. This time one of the mounts got in the way and went down. The other rider urged his horse up onto the boardwalk and came right through the bolted front door in an explosion of shattering wood and glass. Smith dropped the greener and yanked his pistol, a Colt Army revolver, from his belt. He and the ruffian fired simultaneously. The horseman's bullet hit Smith high in the left arm, spinning him halfway around. His bullet caught Cullen's man squarely in the chest. He flipped backwards off his horse, which began to buck and pivot wildly. Shouting and waving his good arm wildly, Smith managed to get it out the door with just a table overturned, goods strewn all over the floor, and a big hole in the main counter.

Checking the gunshot wound, he was relieved to see that it had hit in the fleshy part of his upper arm. It hurt like hell but he knew it would have been hurting a lot more if bone had been shattered. He stuck the Colt Army under his belt and hissed in pain as he tore the sleeve off and wrapped it around the bleeding wound, managing to make a knot with the fingers of one hand and pulling it tight with hand and teeth. Retrieving the greener, he got it open and reloaded, digging two more shells out of a pocket.

Moving to the door, he noticed that the raiders had passed the store and were just then reaching the intersection of Front and Crockett. A crashing din of gunfire came from that direction as the soldiers defending the bank began shooting. Then a bullet plunked into the door frame inches from his face, splinters cutting his cheek open just as he looked left to see if the man whose horse he had downed was still alive. Pinned under the dead mount, the raider was aiming a second shot at him. Smith brought the greener up to hip level and fired both barrels, sending one more of Cullen's killers to meet his Maker.

Looking east down Front Street, Smith decided that all of the raiders had passed his store heading west and into the intersection wrapped in a thick pall of gunsmoke with countless quick flares of light—muzzle-flash. Smith went back through the store and out the back door and looked right. Loomis was standing there in front of a six-mule hitch attached to two freight wagons connected—the tongue of the rear wagon lashed securely with chains and rope to the underside of the front wagon, both wedged into the alley between the general store and the Cigar and Fine Liquor Emporium next door. A half dozen bent wooden bows had been secured to the wagon, to which was secured a sturdy canvas cover.

"Back 'em up!" roared Smith. "Now!"

Loomis unlimbered a bullwhip, stepping away from the lead mules and with a flick of the wrist had the whip snapping above the team, startling the mules. Cursing up a storm, he let fly a few more times, until he had convinced the "goddamned knobheads" to pull back in their traces, and kept at it until the wagons emerged from the alley and stood athwart Front Street. It was impossible for horsemen to go over or between the wagons, and the alleys on both sides were effectively blocked. Then he dropped the bullwhip and grabbed the heart rings that kept the reins straight between the pair of lead mules. Digging in his heels he hollered "Whoa! Whoa damn you!" As hard as it was to get a mule started, it was harder to get them stopped. He pulled until he felt like his arms would fall off, then muttered a grim "Well, hell!" as he let go and backed up and pulled a Walker Colt out of his belt. "Hate to do it, and Stick will prolly skin me alive, but...." He aimed the big horse pistol at the head of the left-hand leader.

And then the mules stopped.

"Well you longears ain't as dumb as you look," Loomis said.

The mule he had been about to shoot made a loud half-whinny, half-braying sound. Loomis went to work unhitching the six-in-hand from the lead wagon.

In the store, John Smith strode back to the front door, reloading the greener one more time. He wondered if Arch Cullen was still alive. Cursing under his breath, and holding his injured arm tight against his side, he went out and walked with long, purposeful strides along the buildings on the south side of Front, heading for the intersection. He had been after The Angel of Death too long to stand by while someone else killed the son of a bitch.

III.

Cord Remington was sheltering behind the sandbag redoubt encircling the roofed boardwalk in front of the bank when the intersection filled with Cullen's mounted killers, and a blistering barrage of bullets began to buzz like hornets around him, thumping into the sandbags and slapping against the lumber in the boarded-up windows and sounding like dozens of pickaxes against rock as they pelted the stone wall of the bank building. Captain Bolt and eight of his soldiers were with him, and a half dozen more were in the bank, firing their single-shot Springfield Trapdoor carbines through the boards slanting across the windows or through the open doorway from further back in the bank.

A soldier right next to him tried to get a shot off but rose up just a little too much – a bullet hole appeared in his forehead and his carcass was hurled backwards. A horse and rider loomed above Cord, the animal's legs colliding with the redoubt. The rider raked the horse with his spurs and the horse hopped over the sandbags. Cord fell on his right shoulder, rolled onto his back and shot the rider out of his saddle, then rolled up against the redoubt in an effort to avoid being trampled as the wild-eyed cayuse pivoted, whinnying shrilly, then jumped back over the redoubt and into the swirling mass of horsemen.

The soldiers hunkered down behind the sandbags began shooting into the mass of riders, while ten more fired through the boards on the windows or from the door. Cord knew it was a matter of time before those with him at the redoubt were overrun. Another horse sailed over the line of sandbags, collided with the front wall of the bank and turned sideways. Its rider shot down into the row of blue-coated men and killed two of them before he slipped off his saddle, riddled with bullets.

A second horse came over the redoubt, slamming into the first and going down on its side, throwing its rider to the boardwalk next to Cord. Stunned by the fall, the raider rolled over, saw Cord, and brought his pistol around. Cord shot him in the face, crawled over him, and got up, pulling the carcass up in front of him, feeling the impact of the bullets striking the dead man as he stumbled backward toward the bank door. Bringing his gun arm up between the upper torso and limp arm of his shield, he emptied his gun, firing four rounds into the mass of horsemen. Reaching the threshold, he tripped and fell, the corpse landing on top of him. He rolled it off to one side and scrambled out of the doorway, just as the redoubt collapsed and the few soldiers that remained alive were trampled under the surge of mounted men and riderless horses.

One of the horsemen came through the doorway, Cord scrambled to his feet, tossed aside his empty Schofield and with a running leap launched himself at the raider. They fell off the far side of the horse in a tangle of arms and legs, but the raider took the brunt of the fall, Cord landing on top of him, whipping one of his knives from under the longcoat and plunging it to the hilt into the man's chest. Wrenching a pistol from the dead man's hand, he rolled out from under the rearing horse and shot the animal in the head, then crawled behind the carcass. From this vantage point he could shoot through the door, and emptied the gun into a raider on foot who came charging through, his piercing Rebel yell audible above the deafening clamor of battle.

Cord reached over the barrel of the dead horse and felt the saddlebags, worked his hand inside and pulled out a couple of fully loaded cylinders. The dead man's pistol was a Whitney 2nd Model. The cylinder was easily removed by turning a switch on the left side of the frame. Such handguns were in high demand during the war, since changing cylinders was a much quicker way to reload than emptying a cylinder and reloading it chamber by chamber. This done, he shot a few more rounds through the open door into the melee outside.

Thanks to the obscuring pall of gunsmoke that hung over the street in the crisp still morning, it was impossible to tell how many of Cullen's men remained mounted, but the shooting at and into the bank was still intense. He began to worry about the outcome of the fight. It seemed likely that Captain Bolt and the soldiers who had manned the redoubt were all dead or about to be. There were five soldiers still alive in the bank, hunkered down at the windows or, in the case of two of them, behind the bank counter. Bolt had stationed seven more behind a redoubt at the back door.

His ears ringing from all the close-range gunfire, Cord couldn't tell if there was any shooting in the alley behind the bank, and he wondered what his chances were if he got up to go back and look. To look, though, he had to lift the bar off the back door. Bullets were thumping into the carcass of the horse behind which he sheltered. He emptied the second cylinder, again shooting through the doorway, then switched to a third cylinder and by then had decided he had to know, regardless of the odds. One of the soldiers at the window shouted that he was almost out of ammunition. That made up Cord's mind. He got to his feet and went around the counter, reaching the door without getting a scratch, with bullets buzzing like a nest of hornets in the building. Lifting the thick wooden bar out of its metal braces, he threw open the back door, pistol at the ready.

What he saw surprised him. The seven soldiers were alive, though one was sitting propped up against the sandbags clutching at his shoulder, blood oozing through his fingers. Several dead ruffians and one dead horse lay out in on north Crockett. A corporal presented himself to Cord and explained that a small group of raiders had ventured round the side of the bank and had been repulsed. "We were afraid we'd miss the rest of the fight, Sir."

"You won't. Come inside and keep your head down."

Once they were inside, Cord barred the door and directed the soldiers to take positions behind the counter where, on a normal day, a teller or two would take care of business with bank patrons. The wounded man was left in the rear of the bank, propped up against the back wall.

The boards nailed over the two front windows of the bank had been so riddled with bullets that they had disintegrated into so much kindling, and of course the glass panes were long gone. Cord could see the street better and now it seemed the thick pall of gunsmoke had thinned a bit as the gunfire lessened.

The determination of Cullen's men to get into the bank hadn't diminished, though. Four of them came through the door, and a fifth spurred his horse through a window, knocking down the boards that remained in place. The horse trampled a soldier, breaking his leg.

The men Cord had retrieved from the alley fired a ragged volley that cut down all but one of the raiders, a bearded mountain of a man who took a dozen bullets to kill. Each one staggered him, but he kept firing his two pistols until the hammers fell on empty chambers. Only then did he go down. The horseman pistol whipped a soldier trying to drag him out of the saddle, then turned his pistol on Cord.

Cord had fired his last bullet into the bearded giant. He reached under his longcoat and with a lightning-fast sweep of the arm threw one of his blades, which caught the horseman in the throat. The raider's trigger finger spasmed, and the bullet plucked at a coattail flaring away from Cord's body as he turned with the throw. The horse reared with a shrill whinny as its dying rider slipped sideways out of the saddle, then turned and loped out the door.

IV.

From the roof of the Longhorn Hotel, Emma had a clear view of Front Street to the east and west and Crockett to the north and south. She could see the wagons moved into position to the east down Front Street and in both directions on Crockett. There were supposed to be a blockade west on Front Street, to prevent Cullen and his men from spreading through town—or running away. The Tonkawa hostler named Stick had been given the task of moving the wagons into place on the west side of the intersection. The hotel itself was locked up; Annie Pritchard had wisely decided to take the night train and spend a few days in Fort Worth. Her door and windows had been heavily boarded over. Emma had gotten inside through a back door that opened into the alley between the Longhorn and the Chinese bath house.

After picking off several of the raiders, Emma began to think something had happened to Stick. She hunkered down behind the hotel's facade, which formed a kind of parapet across the front of the building, reloading her Winchester. Four of the raiders who had come into town across the bridge were still down the street, trading lead with townsmen from two buildings, one on the north side of the street and the other on the south. Emma stood up, the Winchester's butt plate to her shoulder, and with three shots knocked three of them out of their saddles. The fourth one spotted her and threw some lead in her direction, then steered his horse down the alley between the hotel and the building immediately west of it. Emma ran to the western edge of the roof and was about to squeeze off a shot just as the rider steered his horse around the back of the land agent's office next door.

What troubled Emma was that Stick and the wagons were in the next alley over, and that was the direction the ruffian had turned.

She didn't hesitate. Putting the One In A Thousand down, she ran to the east edge of the roof and sprinted westward. The alley was about eight feet wide, and the roof of the adjacent building was a few feet lower than the Longhorn. Emma had her arms back and her body tilting forward as she launched herself into the air, Landing on the other roof with inches to spare, on the balls of her feet with her knees bent, she threw her hands out in front of her and tucked her head as she rolled. Coming up on the run, she whipped her twin Schofields out of the cross-draw holsters.

Shots rang out straight ahead of her, distinguishable from the din of gunfire coming from behind her. Reaching the edge of the roof she caught a glimpse of Stick's legs as he scrambled under a wagon. In the same moment that one of the lead mules in the six-mule hitch went down, Emma fired both pistols and the ruffian who had circled behind the land agent's office somersaulted over the back of his horse, dead before he hit the ground.

Emma holstered the Schofields and jumped, landing in the middle of the canvas tarp that covered the first of the pair of wagons, a drop of about fifteen feet. She heard the canvas rip but she didn't fall through into the wagon bed, instead sliding down the side and landing in a crouch to peer under the wagon at Stick.

"You alright?" she asked with a smile. "Time to get these wagons into the street."

Stick nodded, and she rose and stepped back as he emerged and stood, dusting himself off. "Couple of riders had me pinned down, until someone shot them out of their saddles" He looked at Emma, and then at the dead mule, and grimaced "I'm surprised I only lost the one." Drawing a knife, he went to work cutting the harness strap from the dead animal, then took hold of the first mule and started talking to it in what Emma presumed was his native tongue. Much to her surprise, the mules began to back up in the traces. Slowly, the rear wagon emerged from the alley onto Front Street. Slipping past it, Emma reached the boardwalk in time to see a dozen riders thundering across the bridge. It was Tom Dundee and his cowboys, along with Toby Jukes. They galloped past with guns blazing as they fired into the mass of ruffians now milling around in front of the bank. A couple of them took the time to doff their hats to her. One of them was Will. The other was Jukes. Emma smiled warmly and went back into the alley.

"No need to lose more mules," she told Stick. "It's about to come to an end," and with that she loped around the corner of the land office, heading in the direction of Crockett Street.

V.

The arrival of Dundee and his cowboys turned the tide. Cullen and what was left of his followers, nine in number, turned their horses north up Crockett Street, only to pull up short when they saw that wagons blocked the way. It would have been possible to get around them by going single-file on the boardwalks of the buildings on the west side, but for the fact that the townsmen, smelling victory, had emerged from behind their boarded-up windows and were blocking the way. Their fire emptied two more ruffian saddles. Cullen checked the nearest alleys. They too were blocked by armed townsmen. The citizens of Wolf Creek were closing in for the kill. Cullen shouted at his men to follow him, spun his horse, firing his Smith & Wesson Russian Model into the boards covering what had once been a pair of plate glass windows on the west side of The Palace as he raked the horse beneath him with his spurs. The horse leaped over the boardwalk and with a shrill whinny crashed into the boards, splintering them. A pair of mounted raiders went through the second window in the same fashion.

Cullen gunned down one defender who had been shooting from the window and who was now trying to get out of the way. He shot down another who was running for the cover of the long saloon bar, just as Burl, tossing away an empty pistol in disgust, launched himself as one of the mounted raiders, pulled him out of the saddle and began landing powerful blows with his one good hand that left the raider bloodied and unconscious. Grinning, Cullen shot the bartender in the chest, but Burl didn't go down. Instead he roared like a wild animal, blood lust raging in his eyes, as he lumbered towards The Angel of Death. The latter's horse, pivoting and rearing, got in the way. It also prevented Cullen from shooting Burl again. The ex-prize-fighter dropped a shoulder and barreled into the horse, staggered it, then grabbed Cullen by the leg and dragged him out of the saddle. The horse, snorting, ran off, scattering tables and chairs. Cullen rolled over on his back and put a bullet in Burl's heart as the bartender loomed over him. This time Burl went down to his knees, and was dead before his body toppled forward.

Only two of the raiders remained mounted in the saloon. As he got to his feet, Cullen heard two rifle shots in quick succession. The horsemen were punched out of their saddles by the impact of the bullets that killed them instantly. Their lifeless bodies thumped loudly on the blood-splattered saloon floor. Cullen backed up until he collided with the long mahogany bar. A half dozen riderless and agitated horses were milling around in The Palace, overturning all the furniture that was still upright, and he caught only glimpses of a slender woman with long black hair and wearing a duster, standing on the boardwalk outside the window he had come through, aiming a pair of pistols at him. Cullen debated whether to bring the Russian Model to bear on the woman, but then a stocky, broad-shouldered man wearing a shopkeeper's apron and a bloody makeshift bandage on his left arm came through what was left of The Palace's shattered doors, bringing a sawed-off shotgun to bear on Cullen.

"Drop it or die," said Smith flatly.

Cullen thought about it, but it only took a few seconds of staring into the twin black maws of the greener before he made his decision, and let the Russian Model drop.

Emma came through the gaping window frame, broken glass and shattered wood crunching and crackling under her booted feet. With a few softly spoken words she seemed to get the attention of the horses, which she persuaded to leave the same way they had come in. As she joined Smith, the door to the Red Room, pockmarked with bullet holes, creaked open and Colonel Buckley stuck his head out.

"Is it over?" asked the Wolf Creek mayor.

Emma tilted her head slightly, listening. The guns had fallen silent. "Seems like," she replied. "It's safe to come out now."

Buckley scowled, wondering if that had been sarcasm he detected in

Emma's tone. He threw open the door and the percentage girls, all of them clearly shaken by what had just transpired, slowly ventured out. Several of them rushed to Burl's corpse, and launched into lamentations. Others went to a wounded townsman who lay near one of the front windows. Emma noted that several other townsmen lay dead on the floor of the saloon. Buckley approached Emma and Smith, putting a hand on the pistol in his belt as he stared down at Cullen.

"Is this *him*?" asked Buckley. "Is this Arch Cullen?"

Smith nodded.

"Why didn't you kill him? He is too dangerous to let live!"

"I want to see him hang. I want to see him dancing on the end of the rope in his last few seconds of life. He killed my mother and father at Lawrence. I want to watch him suffer."

Buckley was rubbing his chin thoughtfully. "Arch Cullen hanged in Wolf Creek. That will certainly put us on the map, won't it?"

Emma's eyes were hooded and dark as she glowered at the mayor. "What about all the men—and a woman—who died today to keep this town from being destroyed?" She didn't wait for an answer, touching Smith's arm and then walking out of The Palace.

The intersection of Crockett and Front was blanketed with dozens of dead men, and too many horses for her liking. Several columns of smoke rose from various parts of town, which she assumed to be the product of burning buildings, but she was confident that most of the town had been saved. Her brother's plan had worked. That didn't surprise her.

Dundee and some of his cowboys were still in their saddles, talking to her brother, who stood in front of the bank, surrounded by some blue-coated soldiers. Cord was looking for her, and when their eyes met he grinned from ear to ear and waved. Vastly relieved, Emma waved back, then turned to head east down Front Street with long strides.

"Isn't that your sister?" Dundee asked Cord.

Cord nodded, smiling. "She's off to Alamo Freight, to check on a certain horse she's pretty fond of."

Emma was halfway to her destination when she heard a rider coming up behind her and turned as the cowboy named Will checked his cowpony and touched the brim of his hat, looking very relieved.

"Glad to see you're still above snakes, miss."

"But of course," she replied, smiling up at him as she ran a hand along the sorrel's neck, looking it over from muzzle to fetlock. "Looks like you've got a good one here, Will."

"You remember my name?" he asked, astonished.

"I remember the names of handsome cowboys," she assured him, placing her hand on his leg next.

Will stiffened in the saddle and, stumbling over his words, said, "How's your horse, miss?"

"I'm going now to find out. He's at the Alamo Freight yard."

"If you want, you can climb aboard and I'll...."

She grabbed his belt and in one smooth motion swung up astride the sorrel's croup and put her arms around Will's midsection. The speechless cowboy urged his horse into a lope.

"Any of your friends get hurt?" she asked.

"Monte and Jeb got nicked, that's all."

They reached Alamo Freight a moment later and Emma dismounted and hurried to the gate, which opened for her. As she passed through she looked around and smiled again at Will. When the gate closed, he turned his horse and kicked into a gallop with an exuberant yell.

As Emma entered the freight company compound Longshot came trotting across the yard to meet her. He let her wrap her arms around his neck and whickered.

Jacoby walked over with the bad news about Ned Bohannon. "Anybody else get killed?" he asked.

"Some. But Arch Cullen is in custody and every last one of his men is dead. We won. Wolf Creek is saved. The soldiers get paid."

"Yeah." Jacoby's voice sounded hollow. "Ned was a friend of mine."

"Isn't he still?"

He looked at her, then understood, nodded. "Yes. Yes, he still is." He smiled pensively and walked away.

VI.

The bodies of Cullen's raiders were loaded up in wagons and hauled a few miles west of town, where they were buried in a mass grave. The decision was made to burn the corpses, in order to discourage a sudden infestation of coyotes and turkey vultures.

In the two days after the raid, nine Wolf Creek residents were laid to rest in the cemetery. One of them was Ned Bohannon. Then there was The Palace barkeeper named Burl. Another was the town drunk, Willie, found sitting up against a wall, shot in the head, clutching a half-empty bottle of rotgut. In death he was accepted as a member of the community. The young Irish preacher, O'Clary, was busy from daybreak to dusk. So was the local undertaker, who had to recruit some help to make enough coffins.

Cord attended every service. Emma didn't make a single one. John Smith, with his left arm in a sling, was there to show his last respects, while Toby Jukes kept an eye on Cullen in his cell. Noting how grim Cord was, Smith felt compelled to speak up after the service.

"Not your fault these people are dead, you know."

"They died carrying out my plan. I bear some responsibility."

"It was your plan, yes, and it was a damn good one, too. It saved Wolf Creek. There would be a lot more graves to dig if you and you sister hadn't showed up. And Cullen might have made off with all that money and there would have been hell to pay. I hope you and your sister are well paid. When are you two heading home?"

"Pretty soon. What about you? Going to stick it out here?"

Smith nodded. "I'm starting to like being a storekeeper."

"What about being a Pinkerton man?"

"I've retired. Sent a wire to Allan Pinkerton yesterday. He's coming down to be at Cullen's hanging, of course."

Cord extended a hand and Smith took it—and when the handshake was over he looked at the town marshal's badge Cord had pressed into his palm.

"What gives you the idea I want this?" asked the storekeeper.

"You're the best man for the job."

"The town council will have to decide that."

"If they ever get around to it. But right now, by the authority vested in me, I'm making you Acting Marshal of Wolf Creek, Texas. Don't make me pull out that paper with President Grant's signature on it."

"No, you've been doing that enough." John Smith grinned and closed his big fist around the tin star.

VII.

On the third day after the raid the detail from Fort Griffin arrived, forty men and a wagon, one with supplies, the other to transport the two payroll chests. It was commanded by a Captain Ezra Russell, who was informed that fifteen members of the 18th Infantry had perished in the fight, including Captain Bolt. The bodies had been shipped back to Fort Worth by rail the day before, while the rest of Bolt's command remained to guard the payroll.

Toby Jukes told Cord that Kitty was giving Arch Cullen nine kinds of hell as they sat in separate cells across from each other. It had come to Kitty's attention that Cullen's men had busted into the unguarded jail during the raid and found her there—but didn't get her out. Instead, they tried to burn down the jail with her in it. Apparently, the night before the raid, Cullen had made it clear to his men that he didn't care if his spy survived.

"He is a bad man, sure enough," commented Jukes. "But not a bad judge of character, I reckon."

Cord laughed.

The next morning, he was told that Arch Cullen had hanged himself from the bars of his cell, using a leg of his trousers. Cord was relieved. It was one less snake in the tall grass.

Later that day Cord tried to give Win Bohannon the packhorse he and Emma had brought from Santa Fe, but Win somberly insisted on paying a fair price for it. He was taking over the business of the livery, and it seemed to Cord that he had changed dramatically overnight. Gone was the bashful, exuberant boy full of dreams. Even Emma's presence could not bring a smile to his lips.

That day they loaded their horses into a livestock car and took the Texas & Pacific train to Ft. Worth, destined first for Fort Leavenworth, where they would meet Colonel Bronson. After that they would ride the Atchison, Topeka & Santa Fe to Lamy.

The train station platform was full of people there to see them off. Amos Chelico and John Jacoby and even Colonel Buckley were on hand. Toby Jukes was there, as the acting marshal had hired a couple of townsmen who had proven adept with firearms as deputies while The Angel of Death remained in the town jail.

Emma arrived arm in arm with John Smith, which didn't surprise Cord, since he knew she had not slept in her hotel room bed the previous night. They embraced in a long final kiss.

There was no fanfare, no big send off, and no indication that any of the people gathered there that bright, sunny, and very cold morning were sorry to see them go. No one did any speechifying, though some did shake Cord's hand and tip their hats to Emma.

They had the passenger car to themselves, since it was an eastbound train. Emma sat across the aisle from her brother and stretched her legs out on the bench with a contented sigh. "Why did you decide not to go back the way we came?"

Cord was perusing the latest issue of the *Wolf Creek Chronicler*, which was devoted in its entirety to a recounting of the raid. "For the sake of all the hidehunters out there," he replied. "Besides, we're in no hurry to get back, are we?"

"Well, I thought you might be, since those two women you shipped to Santa Fe will be waiting for you."

He looked at her, surprised. "How did you know?"

"You're not the only detective around here," she replied, with a smirk.

A slender, gray-haired black man in a porter's uniform came through the forward door of the car and approached, bearing a tray raised on one hand at shoulder level. When he reached them, he bent slightly at the waist, smiling warmly at Emma, and lowered the tray so she could see the single glass on it filled with a clear amber liquid.

"Good afternoon, miss. My name is Marsh. I have a Sazerac for you."

"Did you swirl the absinthe in the glass before adding the rest of the ingredients?" she asked.

"Oh, yes, miss, I surely did. I'm from New Orleans, so I know how to make this drink just right."

Emma took the glass and tasted it, then sat back with a look of pure rapture on her face. "Perfect."

"I'll be back soon to see if you would like another, miss," promised the porter, quite pleased, and left the way he had come.

Emma took another sip and glanced across the aisle at her brother. "You did this, didn't you?"

"When we get back to Santa Fe, all your beaus will be spoiling you rotten. I wanted to spoil you a little first, to let you know how happy I am that we do this work together." He went back to perusing the newspaper.

She studied his profile a moment. As the person who knew Cord Remington the best, she had a feeling her attention to John Smith, specifically the nights she had spent with the storekeeper, had forced her brother to contemplate what it would be like if she found something better to do that travel all over the frontier with him solving other people's problems.

A steam whistle presaged a violent jolt as the eastbound train got under way. Emma sat back and sipped the Sazerac. As one who believed that actions spoke louder than words, she decided not to attempt to reassure her brother with earnest assertions that she had no intention of quitting the family business. Rather, she gazed out the window for a while as the train picked up speed and left Wolf Creek behind, then murmured, "This is the life."

Cord glanced at her, and smiled.

THE END

AN EXCERPT FROM THE REMINGTONS # 2

The Dolorosa Women

On the trail of a valuable racehorse thought to have been stolen by the notorious bandit leader called Morado, Cord Remington ends up in a small border town called Dolorosa, waking up one morning to find himself married to not one but two lovely young señoritas.

That turns out to be the least of his problems, as he and all the women in Dolorosa are caught in the middle of a conflict between a ruthless Rurales captain and Morado's murderous *bandoleros*.

Emma Remington rides south when she doesn't hear from her brother when she's supposed to, she rides south—straight into an Apache ambush. Turns out the Apaches hate Morado and want him dead. Only question is, will they let Emma help them or decide to kill her?

Chapter One

Cord Remington woke up with a fearsome headache. He felt like he had been pistol-whipped, or thrown by a horse, or gone ninety rounds with William Miller, the Australian champion in boxing, fencing, wrestling and weight-lifting who had come to the United States two years ago and proceeded to defeat every boxing and wrestling champion around. He had been shucked by an ornery cayuse on occasion, and been knocked upside the head by a pistol barrel a couple of times, but he had not yet been crazy enough to step into the ring with "The Professor"—Miller's moniker—but he was sure his head, at the very least, would be hurting if he had.

Since he couldn't yet remember a single thing that had happened the night before, Cord thought a look around might be helpful. He pried his eyes open but as soon as he did a light so bright it sent a lancing pain through his head made him squeeze his eyelids shut and discouraged him from making further attempts.

He heard voices, so distant it sounded as though they issued from the bottom of a deep well. His nostrils flared and he caught the pungent tangy musk of tequila. And something else. Warm sweaty flesh and desert flowers. He started groping blindly round. His left hand came to rest on the unmistakable curve of a woman's hip. His other hand found a perky breast. Then he was kicked in the shin and heard a woman's sleepy moan and he forced his eyes open by dint of great willpower, blinding light be damned.

He found himself in a small adobe hut measuring about ten feet by twelve, with a single door covered by a blanket. The sun was in just the right place to shine through the space between the blanket and one side of the unframed door and momentarily blinded him as he opened his eyes. To escape this unpleasantness, he managed to get up on an elbow, to discover that he lay on a cornhusk mattress which in turn lay on a frame of timber. He was wedged between two naked young Mexican women. It was their dusky skin that gave off the aroma of flowers and perspiration and tequila and sex. Their legs were entangled with his. He carefully pushed hair out of their faces.

Make that two pretty, naked young Mexican women who bore a striking resemblance to one another.

Laying there a moment, wedged between the lissome sleeping beauties, Cord tried to remember the night before. He put his hands behind his head and decided this was a moment that deserved to be relished. It wasn't every day that a man found himself in such a pleasant situation. He remembered some of it now—riding into a town called Dolorosa, a town out in the middle of nowhere, a few days south of the border between Mexico and the Arizona Territory. Finding the cantina, he drank some tequila, met these two women—who, as he now recalled, said they were twin sisters—and apparently spent the night with them, and a good bit of the morning too, by the looks of it.

Bits and pieces of what had transpired on this makeshift bed the night before came back to him, and he began to entertain a notion. And why not, he asked himself, caressing the long perfect curve of a hip with a sort of reverence one might have for something rare in life. Then the girl stirred, eyelids fluttering, a carnal smile on her lips as she reached for him, still half-asleep, and Cord suddenly felt uneasy. Something wasn't right. For one thing, he had always been able to hold his liquor. Something else nagged at him but he couldn't quite figure out what, in his current befuddled state.

He got to his feet a little too quickly. The fly-specked walls of the adobe began to spin. He stumbled to the doorway and threw the blanket aside, grunting as the bright hot sunlight slanted painfully into his eyes and momentarily blinded him.

He was six feet tall, his body whipcord lean, broad-shouldered and narrow in the hips. His black hair was long overdue a trim. His eyes were his most arresting facial feature. They were the gray-blue of a high mountain lake on a cloudy winter's day.

Those eyes temporarily blinded, Cord leaned heavily against the nearest wall, felt the sudden need to relieve himself and gave in to it. While listening to his stream splatter on the hardpack beneath the cedar *ramada* attached to the front of the adobe, he heard women whisper and giggle and that made his vision clear in a hurry. Several of them were carrying baskets of laundry down a sloping path in front of the adobe, towards a shallow stream nearby. They were staring at him, murmuring between themselves. Cord grabbed the nearest thing with which to cover himself—the blanket serving as the adobe's crude door.

"Por favor perdone mí, señoras," he mumbled.

They giggled and chattered about him some more and hurried along, saying things that should have flattered him. But he looked around for his bay gelding and didn't see it, and that was worrisome. Cord retreated inside and spied his belongings thrown on and under a small table in the corner. His tried-and-true Spencer carbine was propped in a corner in its saddle boot. He pulled on his brown canvas pants and then sat on a stool to get his tall stovepipe boots on, tucking the trouser legs into them. He straightened up to find himself face to face with the pert little breasts of one of the disheveled young vixens who draped her arms over his shoulders and her legs and bare derriere across his lap.

"You are not leaving us are you, Señor?" she asked, pouting.

He was sorely tempted by the scent of her, the heat from her body, the weight of her in his lap, and knew that if he gave in to temptation he would spend the rest of the day in the adobe. Then he spent another minute trying to figure out why that would be a bad thing. There was that little matter of finding the stolen thoroughbred named Galileo, who was the most valuable horse in North America. While his present situation made it apparent that his personal morality was sometimes questionable, he did have a strong work ethic, and he had taken on the job of finding a stolen horse and he knew his conscience would begin bothering him if he spent an entire day in the company of the twins.

"No," he replied, and slid her off his lap to stand, grabbing a small sack of coin he had left in his boot overnight. "But first I need to find my horse."

"Your *caballo* is tied in front of the *cantina*," she said, moving closer, running fingers through his chest hair. "I will go with you."

Cord chuckled, looking her up and down. "You'll go to the cantina like that?"

She shrugged, a saucy smile on her lips. "If it bothers you, I will put something on."

"Doesn't bother me." He donned a shirt of oft-mended, sun-faded blue cotton twill, then buckled his gun-belt round his waist and checked the .45 loads in the cylinder of Smith & Wesson Schofield. It was habit, and he did it every time he wore the pistol. His two custom made Arkansas Toothpicks, perfectly balanced for throwing, were sheathed on the back of his hips. Stuffing his shirt tail into his pants he muttered, "Can't believe I left my horse and saddle behind...." then glanced at her and grinned ruefully, "but I guess I had my mind on other things. What's your name?"

"Florita." She wore a faded and oft-mended peasant's dress, and gasped as he grabbed her and tossed her over his shoulder before walking outside, keeping an arm locked firmly down across the back of her thighs to keep her in place, carrying his carbine in the other hand. Pausing in the striped shade of the ramada, he glanced left and down the path to see a half-dozen women washing clothes in a shallow stream. Across the stream were some wind-warped cottonwoods clinging precariously to life, and beyond these an expanse of desert, and beyond that a blue line of mountains which he knew to be the Sierra Madre.

That was where it was generally believed that the notorious bandit Juan Morado was hiding out.

He turned uphill, taking the path that led past other adobe huts on his right. To his left was a low stone wall lined by more cottonwoods, and beyond this, between the wall and the creek, some cultivated fields. About fifty yards further along, a square opened up on the right, a well at the center, a small chapel and the cantina facing each other. More huts were scattered over the rocky slope above these structures and at the top of the hill stood a two-story structure that had the look of a small adobe blockhouse.

All of this he saw clearly for the first time, in full daylight, as he had arrived in Dolorosa after nightfall. But none of it warranted more than cursory interest even now, because his focus was on the bay gelding tethered to a cedar post in front of the cantina. The saddle was still there, the saddlebags too. Having expected the worst, he was pleasantly surprised and much relieved.

The horse whickered happily as he approached. Cord shrugged Florita off his shoulder and stood her on the ground, tied his Spencer rifle in its boot to his rig, and proceeded to check the saddlebags just to make sure his belongings were still there.

"My people may be poor but they would not steal your things," said Florita solemnly. "Bandits will steal you blind. Some Federales and Rurales too. And the Apache who live up in the mountains, they will take everything from you, including your dignity and your life. But not my people."

Cord looked across his saddle at her, standing there barefoot and disheveled, her dress having slipped off one shoulder, and looking very serious. "You're right. I shouldn't have worried."

A portly man with an overgrown mustache concealing a few of his jowls emerged from the cantina, squinting against the bright sunlight. He glanced at Cord, nodded, then looked at Florita and the two of them shared the knowing smile of two people who shared a secret. Then the man threw out his arms in effusive welcome. "*Señor*! So good to see you again!"

Cord brandished four bits from the small sack of coins and put it in the man's beefy palm. "That's for watching out for my cayuse."

The cantina owner was nonplussed. He had not been watching out for the bay gelding at all, as he believed that nothing people left outside his establishment were his responsibility. This sometimes extended to things *inside* the cantina, too, usually when guns or knives were being brandished and his life or own property was in jeopardy. But like all good businessmen he quickly shed any scruples he might have had and nodded to Cord, his hand closing possessively around the money. "I was very happy to do it, *Señor*, and glad that I could be of service," he said gravely, as though he had been dutifully devoted throughout the night to the guardianship of all of the *gringo's* belongings. Then, as a courtesy, he added, "My name is Ochoa, in case you drank a little too much tequila." He winked.

Cord had the sudden urge to get on his high horse and ride out of Dolorosa right then. He couldn't have put into words why he felt that way. The feeling that he had overstayed his welcome was one he usually heeded. He stood there a moment, indecisive, glancing from Florita to the bay, who was nodding his eagerness to be on the move after a long night tied to a pole with no grass to graze or oats to eat. Cord was trying to decide whether he wanted to find out what these two people knew that he didn't know.

Then he saw Florita's sister coming up the road. He spent a moment trying to recall her name before realizing it was an exercise in futility. She wore a dress, the same pale yellow cotton dress she had been wearing last night in the cantina. It occurred to him then that the dresses worn by a female peon, especially younger ones, were considerably more revealing than anything an Anglo woman would ever wear in public. They were sleeveless, low-necked and extended only to the calves. Made that way, they were far more practical for the climate than what a woman would wear in, say, San Antonio, where not even the soiled doves would show a bare calf, and respectable women wore long skirts with petticoats beneath, and long-sleeved blouses that buttoned at the throat.

When she was closer, Florita's sister broke into a run, a salacious smile on her lips, and leaped at Cord so that he had no choice but to grab her in his arms to prevent her from falling. She planted a flurry of hot wet kisses all over his face.

"I was afraid," she exclaimed, once she had come up for air, "that you had gone away! Then I told myself that he would not do such a thing. Not after what happened last night."

Cord smiled politely, glancing sidelong at the Ochoa and praying that the woman didn't launch into graphic details in front of the man. "Well, truth be known, I do have to get going. I'm down here for a reason, you see. ..."

Florita's sister pouted and wrapped her legs more tightly around his midsection.

Ochoa tilted his head, looking puzzled. "You are really leaving, *señor*? After what happened last night?"

Startled, Cord peered at the man, wondering if was trying to be funny, since he thought Ochoa was referring to his night-long frolic with the sisters. But Ochoa appeared to be quite serious, even concerned. "Well, yes, much as I hate to. I mean they work in your cantina. I just assumed, you know, that they were whores. No offense, ladies. I paid them already, so now seems like a good time to get back to work."

"But *señor*!" The cantina owner stood there, arms outstretched, palms up. "But *señor*! They are *putas*, yes, but you married them anyway! And now you are going to leave them to fend for themselves?"

Cord stared at him, incredulously. "Say *what*?"

"*Si, señor, es verdad.* You became so fond of Florita and Anita that you wanted to marry them. If only you could recall how happy they were when they heard you say that! So I sent for the priest. At first he said you would have to pick one or the other, since pal.... pol...." The *cantina* owner's bristly brows came together as he tried to remember the word.

"Polygamy," said Cord flatly.

"*Si, si! Poligamia.* He said the Church frowns on *poligamia*. But the girls talked him into it. They told him that they have always lived together and could not stand being apart from one another, and that they had always shared, which meant that if he did not let you marry them both then one of them would have to be an adulteress, so it would be his fault if one of them burned in the everlasting fires...."

While Ochoa spoke, Cord pried Anita's arms from around his neck and let her down. "*Entiendo*," he said. "Problem is, I have a job to do." Stunned by the *cantina* owner's claim that he had married the sisters, he quickly decided that the owner—and no doubt the sisters, too—were accomplices in some sort of confidence game. "You see, I'm looking for a horse. Sorrel with two stockings, left front and right back legs. Stands about seventeen hands high. Did I not ask you if you had seen such a horse when I came into your cantina last night?"

"Why are you looking for a horse, *Señor*? You have a horse."

"This one is a very special horse," Cord assured him.

The cantina owner shook his head. "No, *Señor*. All you asked was if I had tequila—and a whore."

Cord shook his head. That didn't sound at all like something he would say.

Florita was no longer looking happy. In fact, she stood there with fists planted on her nicely flared hips, staring stonily at Cord. "He thinks we planned this so that he would have to buy his way out," she said, addressing Ochoa.

Cord nodded and smiled. There was more to Florita than just a sex-hungry siren. "You're right. That's what I believe," he said.

"But it's not true." she said, earnestly.

"Let us all go inside," suggested Ochoa. "We will have a drink and talk this over."

"Coffee, strong and black, is all I'm drinking" vowed Cord. He gestured for the sisters to enter the cantina first, and followed them along with the owner, taking the Spencer out of the saddle boot and bringing it with him. It wasn't that he expected violence. But as recent events had just born out, one could never tell what might happen....

Find out more about The Remingtons and the West they lived in, as well as sneak peeks at upcoming books in the series at jason-manning.weebly.com/the-remingtons.html

About the Author

JASON MANNING is the author of numerous frontier novels. A member of SHEAR, the Society for Historians of the Early American Republic, he has a master's degree from Stephen F. Austin State University, specializing in the early national and antebellum periods of American history. He is also an advocate for the protection and recovery of wolves and other endangered species in the United States. He and his family live in the historic town of Nacogdoches, Texas.

www.ingramcontent.com/pod-product-compliance
Lightning Source LLC
Chambersburg PA
CBHW060554100726
47907CB00005B/1360